COFFEE

COFFEE

RACHEL L. SANDERS

Charleston, SC
www.PalmettoPublishing.com

COFFEE
Copyright © 2023 by Rachel L. Sanders

All rights reserved
No portion of this book may be reproduced, stored in a retrieval system, or transmitted in any form by any means–electronic, mechanical, photocopy, recording, or other–except for brief quotations in printed reviews, without prior permission of the author.

First Edition

Paperback ISBN: 979-8-8229-2025-5

DEDICATION

This book is dedicated to my mother, Ethel. Mom was a storyteller and a serious coffee drinker. Many nights, she would drink her coffee and tell one of her intriguing stories about her childhood in Louisiana. She would have the neighborhood children sitting on our front porch listening to the stories that she told. A few of those children would become so frightened that they would require someone to walk them home—even if their home was only three doors down, but they always came back for more. Mom always told me that I was just like her; she always said that I had a creative mind, and she would encourage me to put my stories on paper. Therefore, I take this time to thank her and to dedicate this book, *Coffee*, to her even though she is no longer with me physically. She and her words of encouragement have forever stained my heart.

I love and miss you, Mom.

—The baby of the bunch

PROLOGUE

Temple, TX
July 6, 2017

"Hello, Pastor, thank you for coming all the way here to speak with me. It's been a long time coming, and I'm not sure where to turn. Things have become so out of place lately. I don't know how much more I can take."

"Not a problem. What are the doctors saying? Have they provided a diagnosis and prognosis yet? Well, before we get started, why don't you start by sharing with me exactly what you have been experiencing."

COFFEE

"Well, Pastor, I sure hope that you have time. Because in order for me to provide you with a clear explanation of what I've been experiencing, I must take you all the way back to the beginning. But in the meantime, would you like a cup of coffee?"

Temple, TX
August 23, 2016

This is the reason why I'm breaking up with him: the time is now 11:23, and he was to meet me here at 10:30 for coffee. I know, I know…why am I continuing to wait and he's almost an hour late? I ask myself the same question, and the answer is because I am determined to do this, it is over. And I must tell him. Here he comes now, walking as if he's not late or that I haven't been sitting here for a while. The look on his face shows me that he has no care or urgency in meeting me here.

"Hey, babe, sorry I'm late. I had business to take care of."

I'm sure he can see the rage and steam beaming from my nostrils and my ears.

"Paul, you're an hour late. Why didn't you text me to inform me that you would be late?"

Looking at his phone as if it is the love of his life, Paul says to me, "I'm here, aren't I? Stop complaining so much. No man wants a complaining woman. Order something so we can get out of here. Besides, I have good news to share with you."

He says this as if I care. At this point I don't care if Paul would tell me that he won a million dollars. I'm so fed up with him and his arrogant and narcissistic ways, breaking up with him is my only option.

The whole while I'm looking at him with great disgust and thinking to myself, *This is the moment, Sam. Tell him. You can't back out now.* Therefore, I take a deep breath, and I look directly into Paul's once-big, beautiful eyes that I now look at as being the eyes of none other than the devil himself, and I say to him, "Paul, we need to talk."

Paul is so dismissive and uninterested in what I have to say. He ignores my comments, interrupts me as usual, and blurts out, "I'm so excited. I will be leaving the country to study abroad…"

My initial reaction was to jump up and down: to celebrate him leaving because I wouldn't have to deal with his bull anymore. But he's so pompous, so self-centered and ego driven, that I allow my arrogance and anger to manifest its way to the top of my to-do list and take control. The need to deflate Paul's puffed-up ego has become the center of this very moment, and while Paul is celebrating within

COFFEE

himself, I'm contemplating on just the right time and the right words to burst his bubble. And as soon as he finishes displaying his hubristic belief in his own self-proclaimed bravura, I give it to him. I let loose, and it comes pouring out. I give in to my selfish flesh, and I exhale the words that I have been censoring. I let out the words that have been eating away at me for months now: those harsh words that I know would devastate him, those words that could bring Paul's life down like an imploding building. Those four words are here. They have come from a deep-seated place and now are on the tip of my tongue, ready to make their debut. I open my mouth like a curtain on a theater stage, and the words come out past the proscenium arch of my mouth, and I say:

"Paul, it is over."

Paul is looking away from me and never flinches. Instead, he continues to stare out of the window, then down at his watch as if he has somewhere to be. The silence that sits between the two of us is exasperating. I can feel the knot in my throat building in anticipation of what he's going to say, as I'm thinking, *Say something you idiot. I know you heard me.* As quickly as the confidence built for me to let him have it, the guilt of what I'd just said is building even quicker. The regret is forming in my throat like foam. My heart is racing. My hands are trembling as I clear my throat. I'm thinking, *Why am I feeling guilty?* I don't know; am I going to apologize? *Hell no. So, Sam get a grip*, I say to myself.

And then it happens. Paul's response is not what I expected. I did expect him to be angry because he can't accept rejection, but I'm looking at him as the frown lines on his forehead are becoming more pronounced. Paul's level of anger is beyond even the norm for him, but my concern for his unusual air of quietness is predominate. Paul looks over to his left, peering around the coffee shop. I'm wondering if he's looking for someone. Is someone supposed to meet him here? As Paul continues to look around, the look on his face is a bit stoic, but I can see the veins popping from his forehead showing the level of wrath and indignation within. He then turns his attention back toward me, the neophyte I had become in speaking my mind, and he begins to stare at me. Paul has never been aggressive toward me, so I'm not worried about that, but it's something in his eyes that confirms to me that I'm making the right decision. But my decision may have caused me a bit of a problem; therefore, to break the silence and uncomfortableness that we're both experiencing, I say to him,

"Paul, did you—"

Paul aggressively interrupts me by saying: "You will never leave me, do you f*cking understand? Do you?"

COFFEE

Paul says this at the same time the waiter is coming to our table to take our order. The waiter looks over to say something to Paul, and Paul immediately says, "Man, get the hell away from here."

The waiter stops in his tracks and looks over at me. The waiter is just as confused as I am. He then looks at Paul, then looks back over at me as I give him a slight shaking of my head to express my level of disgust and disagreement with Paul's behavior. Then as soon as the waiter is out of sight and no one else is around, Paul jumps up and slams his fist down on to the table so hard that it causes my cup of coffee to spill out. He then walks away. Just when I think I can relax because I'm finally free from him, Paul rushes back toward me, takes his index finger, and pokes me very harshly in the center of my forehead. The poke is so hard that my head jerks back from the force, and with a scowling look and demanding tone, Paul says, "You will regret this, *I promise*." And he hurriedly walks out of the coffee shop, and just like that, I exhale thinking, *Paul is out of my life… for good.*

CHAPTER ONE

Temple, TX
August 24, 2016

As I'm walking down the stairs, I call out to Mom, "Mom, I'm all packed and ready to go."

But there was no answer. I should have known at that time that something wasn't right with her because Mom is an early riser, especially on the days when I have to return to campus. Therefore, I call out to her again, "Mom, do you hear me?"

As I turned to walk into the dining room, I see strewn across the dining room table, papers, papers, and more papers. Mom's head is down on the table…

aw, she's tired. I must have kept her up too late packing. I walk up and tap Mom on the shoulders, and she doesn't move. I'm thinking, *Wow, is she asleep? That's not like her.*

"Mom, wake up. I'm about to get back on the road. I want to make it back to school to see Mrs. Audria Voltsclaw, my design instructor."

Mrs. Voltsclaw was such a bore, but the woman knew her stuff. She was a very tall Austrian woman who was married to a Russian: crazy match-up. I remember when I first stepped into her class, I thought her to be German, as tall as she was. Talking to her was so hard because she talked very slow. I understood that part of it was because she had a very strong accent and wanted to ensure others understood her. I cringe when I talk longer than two minutes to her. Any time longer than that would cause my mind to slip into my own burrow to escape the pain of having to listen to her. I would begin imagining ways to slap her in the mouth with a wet dish rag. Mom would share stories from back in her days of believing that slapping people with a wet dish rag would help with their speech impediments, but this only worked for people that had stuttering problems, and I knew it to be nothing more than one of Mom's many fairytales. But at the rate I was going with Mrs. Voltsclaw, I was willing to take a chance, otherwise risk not hearing anything she said. Therefore, with Mom's story being a fable and knowing that hitting her was far beyond reality, I settled for recording her classes. It was the only way that I could obtain the valuable information that she was sure to put out during my time of mentally checking out. I would have to admit, she knew her design and style; she also knew a lot of fashion designers. I never understood why she refused to submit her ideas to any of her fancy designer friends.

As I tap Mom on the shoulder, the touch of her body tells me without a doubt that Mom's sleeping was involuntary.

"Mom, are you ok? Mom, Mom!"

Mom doesn't respond. Her body was a bit limp, and I knew at that time my mommie was in trouble. I immediately take my cell phone out of my back pocket and dialed 911.

"This is the 911 Operator, how may I help you?"

"I need an ambulance to 526 Ethels Avenue. Hurry, my mom is unresponsive."

"Is she breathing?"

"Yes, she's breathing, but she won't wake up. This isn't like her."

"Ok, an ambulance is on the way."

"Thank you. Please hurry."

So much went through my mind as I stood there holding my mother's head in my arms thinking, *Mom, what has happened? What's wrong?* My mother is the strongest woman that I know. She has been through so much just so that I could live a decent life. My Father, her ex, walked out on us when I was a small child. When Mom told him that she was expecting a child, he said that he was too young to be a father; however, he stayed around playing dad long enough to where I was able to appreciate his presence. But one day he decided that being a father was no longer at the top of his agenda. In fact, my aunt Sheila, his sister, once told Mom that he said that being a father was cramping his style. He no longer wanted us as a family, and he no longer wanted to be a father; therefore, he walked away and never came back again. No warning, no conversation about why. No goodbye, not even a note. He walked out of our lives and left us for good. It was horrible at first, but after some time, Mom did what she had to do. We struggled, but she tightened her bootstraps, put on her big girl panties, and got a second job. Since then, the two of us have been living our best, never looking back.

The ambulance arrives, and as they are checking her vitals, Mom begins to mumble something, and the paramedic says "She's coming around."

You would've thought that I was told that I had won the lottery from the way I reacted. Mom opened her beautiful, brown eyes, and she's looking dazed and confused. Knowing Mom, she's probably trying to figure out who these people are in our home. Mom was big on not having a lot of people in our home unless she knew them. As a child, I couldn't bring friends to the house without her permission. Mom would want to know who the child was and who the child's parents were. That was Mom. I immediately rush over to her side, grabbing a hold of her hand.

"Mom, it's ok; I am here."

Mom looks up at me and nods as the paramedics place her in the ambulance and pull off. I grab my purse and hop into my car. Nowadays no one is allowed to ride in the back of the ambulance; you must follow them to the hospital of their choice. I follow the ambulance as their sirens are blaring and their speed is picking up. I'm trying hard to think positive and to avoid a personal pity of worry. But my mind continues to go back over some of Mom's behaviors, and I realize, *Mom has been very tired lately, not staying up late watching movies with me, not eating as much. I'm sure it's just dehydration. She's a tough cookie. She will come around. Maybe she's a bit overwhelmed with work and getting me prepared to go back to school. That's all it is, nothing more.*

CHAPTER TWO

Baylor University
September 3, 2016

A text comes in from Mrs. Voltsclaw. *Samantha, come see now.* I knew what it meant. I always thought it was funny that she texted and emailed exactly the way she talked. After being in her class for so long, I understood her broken English and her way of communicating. Many would think it to be rude, but I never perceived her as being rude. It was just the difference in culture.

I look at my text, and I respond with: "Ok, heading your way."

COFFEE

I arrive in Mrs. Voltsclaw's office, and she's in there with Sonny, an up-and-coming design student that has plenty of pazazz. Sonny identifies as being non-binary, and prefers to be addressed as "they," which I have yet to understand. People have said that he identifies this way because he does not conform to the traditional beliefs of gender, but Sonny is in the process of becoming completely transgendered. Sonny has been undergoing therapy to become a female. They were born Jason Platt but go by the name Sonny Platt. I don't care one way or another. Sonny is cool, dresses the part, and can design the hell out of a dress. You want a prom dress, call Sonny. You want a wedding dress, call Sonny. Whatever dress you desire, Sonny is your person, just call Sonny. Sonny has been on campus one year and in that short time they have made a great name for themself. Sonny is so confident in the direction that they are heading that when they are talking about themself, they speak almost entirely in illeism, referring to themself in the third person.

Mrs. Voltsclaw sees me standing at the door waiting on her and Sonny's conversation to end.

"Enter dear," she says, her hand beckoning for me to come in.

Sonny turns around and sees me and says with excitement "My dearie!"—a name they have given me without asking—walking toward me while tossing their long, purple-and-white-printed chiffon scarf around the side of their neck. In their normal, lovely, endearing way, they sashay over to the door and kiss at my left cheek and then at my right. It's Sonny's way of saying hello, and I've gotten so used to it now that when they do it, my mind gives me a quick snapshot of what it would feel like if I traveled to Paris.

"Mrs. Voltsclaw, you texted for me to come see you?"

"Indeed, I did," she says.

I take a seat in the chair facing Mrs. Voltsclaw, and she hands me a white envelope that is addressed to me but with her listed as "In Care Of." Looking curiously at her, I slowly reach to take the envelope from her hand. My eyes are asking what it is without my saying a word, and she shoves it closer and says "open, yes."

Anticipation builds, while excitement yields because I have no way of knowing what is in the envelope. I'm thinking, *Surely, I couldn't be failing her class. What could this possibly be?* I take the envelope and pull out the letter that was inside and read.

Samantha Scott,

We here at the Aalto University of Arts, Design, and Architecture would like to congratulate you on your acceptance to our AU

COFFEE

Helsinki Finland Study Abroad Program and Dress Design Competition. Your application was selected from among several bright and talented designers such as yourself. We extend this offer to you, and it is our hope that you would accept our offer by September 16, 2016. We look forward to hearing from you.

Gasping for air with my hand covering my heart, as if it was going to fall out of my chest, I look at Ms. Voltsclaw and I say to her "Is this for real?"

All the while, I'm thinking, *That's less than two weeks.*

"Why wouldn't it be?" She says while standing and clapping her big hands with those extra-long and narrow fingers together.

She extends her hands for me to give her a hug and I surrender, giving her the biggest hug possible. It was then that I realized that all the questioning she was doing, the pushing me to hurry up and add my final touches to my dress design, was all being done with a hidden agenda. Everything that she had been doing was because my instructor Mrs. Voltsclaw—slow-talking Voltsclaw—had taken it upon herself to submit my dress design and application on my behalf.

Excited and overwhelmed, I say to her "How can I thank you?"

Providing me with a smile that shows that she believes in me, she says, "Go and be great, and don't forget about me."

Shocked that I understood her perfectly, I nodded, looked up at her, and said "I will, and I won't."

The amount of excitement that I was experiencing was like fire going through my bones. It was tantalizing to say the least; I've never felt so ecstatic in my life.

"I must call my mother. She's going to be—"

I stop what I was saying. The thought that invaded my mind was, *Mom will be sad, I reckon. But surely, she will also be proud, right?*

"Mom is going to be so proud of me, I must call her."

Mrs. Voltsclaw shews me away with her hands saying, "Go call Mommy, go, now."

Ring, ring, ring. Mom isn't picking up her phone; therefore, I decide to send her a text telling her to call me. I didn't want to say "immediately" or anything like that because I didn't want to scare her. So, I just said, "Call me when you can."

Time continues to tick away, and I'm still on cloud nine. I have yet to share the great news with Mom, and I don't want to contact other family members or friends until I speak with her. She must be the first to know. Mom is my best friend; she's my G.O.A.T. (Greatest of All Time). We have done

COFFEE

so much together. Every year she and I are sure to take a vacation together, usually to the Caribbean because we both are water hogs, but last year we did something different. We went to Bar Harbor, Maine to visit Cadillac Mountain in Acadia National Park. This is the first point where the sun hits in the United States, so Mom and I wanted to experience such magnificent occurrence. It was another box to check off on our bucket list, not to mention that doing so allowed us to encounter some of the best lobster and crab that could ever grace our lips. The succulency and sweetness are beyond what we would ever experience here at home.

Mom and I talk every day on the telephone. It has been just the two of us all my life, which is why I'm excited and nervous at the same time. Mom works from home, and I will ask her to come to Finland with me. Finland is far away; it's not like being up here at Baylor where she can just hop in the car and come to visit. Nor will I be able to hop in the car to go visit her. No, there is no other way: she'll have to come with me.

It's getting late in the evening, and Mom still hasn't called. I'll try her again; she can't be *that* busy.

Sonny comes running with their arms stretched out and this unusual high-pitched voice saying "Girly, girly, girly, you *go* girl! Sonny is *so* proud of you, my dearie. You go to Finland and do your thing missy, but don't get too comfortable because Sonny Bunny is right behind you." They are saying this while doing their normal kiss to each of my cheeks.

"Thanks Sonny, I appreciate you."

"You? Appreciate Sonny? Get out of here." They say while placing their hand on their heart, and they begin to walk away saying, "You? The design guru? Appreciate Sonny—I must."

Sonny then runs off down the hall like they have just ended a scene in a Broadway stage play. It would not be a surprise to me if later in life I would hear that Sonny eventually explored some form of an acting career because they have a knack for it. I'm standing there, watching Sonny walk off engulfed in their charades, when my phone rings. It's Mom! I can't wait to answer. I'm so excited that I almost hit decline.

Excitedly I answer. "Hello, Mom! Where have you been? I've been trying to reach you!"

But instead of hearing Mom's voice, what I hear on the other end of the telephone is: "Sam, this is Ms. P., your neighbor. I have your mom's telephone. You need to come home quickly, your mom is in the hospital."

CHAPTER THREE

Temple, TX
September 3, 2016

I arrive at the hospital to see Mom hooked up to all kinds of machines. At first glance I didn't recognize her. She was lying in the bed with a blood pressure monitor that was constantly beeping. There was a tube in her mouth connected to an apparatus that was helping her to breathe. Ms. P., our neighbor, comes out of the restroom while I was standing there. Ms. Priscilla Perry is her name. We call her Ms. P. for short. She's a sweetheart at first sight, but she tends to be the one that says "I don't gossip" while she's telling you all the gossip. She, too, is a single mother who raised three children—Michael, Yvonne, and Daisy—who are now in college. Daisy is named after her grandmother and hates her name. Who in their right mind names children "Daisy" in this century? So, Daisy tells everyone that her name is Daisia. Their home is directly next door to ours; we used to play together when we were smaller. Now that we all have went away to college, Mom and Ms. P. seemed to have become closer than ever, which is good because I'm sure they both are lonely, and having each other brings a bit of comfort for them.

"Samantha, I'm so glad that you were able to make it. Your mom always said that if something happened to her to contact you."

"I appreciate it Ms. P., but what happened? What is wrong with my mother?"

"They won't tell me everything, but the one doctor did say that she was bad off. Did you know that your mother had cancer?" Ms. P. asked.

The feeling of utter shock swept through my body when I realized the words that were coming out of Ms. P.'s mouth.

"No, my mother doesn't have cancer; she's in perfectly good health. Where did you get that from Ms. P.? Did the doctor say that?"

Shrugging her shoulders while her hands are still in her pants pockets, she says, "Well, when one of the doctors came into her room, under his name tag was the word *oncologist*. He must be here because she has cancer."

I truly appreciate Ms. P., but she gets under my skin with all of her made up stories without any facts. I can't allow what she says to get to me. I won't. I'll wait until the doctors come in so I can hear what they are saying. I want to tell Ms. P. to go home and that I can take it from here, but I know that if I do, when Mom wakes up, Ms. P. will tell her that I sent her away, and Mom will not be happy. Ms. P. has good intentions, but she's so annoying. So instead I say, "I truly thank you Ms. P. for being here. If you need to go home for a while, I understand. I'll stay with my mom."

"Oh no, honey bear, I'm not going anywhere," she says. Besides, we need to know what's wrong with Sharon. Finding her that way really messed me up. I need a drink now."

I lift my head up from my phone and said, "you found her?"

"Yes. I stopped by the house, and the door was cracked. It looked like she was heading out of the door when it happened. Whatever it may be, she was lying on the floor, car keys still in her hand. She was breathing but wasn't talking. I was terrified. I called her name several times. I said, 'Sharon, Sharon, girl. Sharon, get up!' But I couldn't wake her, so I called the paramedics. They got to the house pretty fast. It was a white guy and an Asian guy. When they got

COFFEE

out, I could tell that the white guy was the real paramedic and the—"

I interrupt Ms. P. because she can go all around the mulberry bush to explain one simple thing. "I get it, Ms. P., so she wasn't talking or anything?"

"No, honey bear, no. She was just lying there and—"

The doctor walks in, and I'm thinking, *Saved by the bell*.

"Hello, I'm Doctor Matthews; I'm the attending physician. Who do we have here?"

"Hello, I'm Samantha, Sharon's daughter, and this is our neighbor. How's she doing? What's wrong with her?"

"Your mother was brought in through emergency. She was unresponsive. While reading her chart, I noticed that the same thing happened a few weeks ago. I called her oncologist, and he will be coming down soon."

Shocked at what the doctor was saying to me, I say, "Oncologist?"

While I am still grasping what the doctor was saying, Ms. P. goes into her own rant, she's wailing her arms in the air and saying, "I knew it! I knew it. Oh, no no, I knew it! I told you! Sharon, no Sharon, don't die on your daughter! We need you!"

I quickly stop what I was saying, and—possibly with too much force or aggression—I say to her,

"Ms. P., *please* let him finish." It was a bit much because Ms. P. and the doctor looked at me as if I were a mad woman. I then say, "Sorry, go on doctor."

I say this while I walk over to Ms. P. and put my arms around her, indicating that I'm aware that I was a bit brash. My hug is expressing contriteness for my actions.

She says, "It's ok, Sam. I know you are upset. That's your mom, and—"

I interrupt her by saying, "Yes, that's my mom. Sir, please, what's wrong with her?"

Dr. Matthews begins to explain to me what is going on with Mom when another doctor walks in. He's the total opposite from what Dr. Matthews looks like. He comes in, he's not wearing a white coat, but he does have a name tag on the left pocket of the white dress shirt that he's wearing. He has a long tie on that I didn't immediately notice that had the word *oncology* written on it. He nods at Dr. Matthews, turns toward me, and says, "Hello, I am Dr. Agelwalabe. I am your mother's oncologist."

CHAPTER FOUR

Temple, TX
September 16, 2016

The sounds of the birds chirping are pleasing to my ears. I lie there for another ten minutes, knowing that the alarm clock will go off in about thirty minutes. It's six in the morning, and I'm not used to being up this early. But I must get up to give Mom her medications and see to it that she has something to eat. Thoughts are running through my mind. I look over at the clock, and it's 6:22 a.m. already. I turn the alarm clock off since I am already awake, but when I look at the clock, I noticed the date, it's September 16th. I stare up at the ceiling thinking,

COFFEE

Today is the deadline to give AU Finland my answer to whether I'll be attending school abroad. As much as I want to say yes, I can't. I can't leave Mom now. She's very sick. Her cancer is advanced and has metastasized. Even though she's taking treatments, she's not doing well with them.

The tears begin to flow from my eyes; my emotions are all over the place. Just two weeks ago, I was celebrating with Mrs. Voltsclaw and Sonny, and now I'm home, caring for my mom who I never told that I had been accepted. I'm angry, but I am also sad. I grab my cell phone from my nightstand to text Mrs. Voltsclaw. I gave no thought to the time of day.

I text: *Mrs. Voltsclaw, I want to thank you for everything that you have done for me over the years. I totally appreciate you for helping me to get accepted into AU; however, I will be notifying them today that I will have to graciously step aside and allow someone else to fill that spot for now. I wanted you to know my decision first before anyone else because I owe you that much. Thanks again.*

As I stand up to prepare for the day, I hear a *ding*. I pick my phone back up, and to my surprise, Mrs. Voltsclaw has responded right away. It's a long text that I'm guessing she had prepared already and was just waiting to hit send. *Samantha, I truly understand. With your gift, there will be other opportunities for you. Please do not feel like you have let me down.*

Know that I am proud of you. Your mother is your first priority, as she should be. You do what you must do, and we will look forward to you returning and getting back in full swing. I ask of you this: let's not decline the offer, but instead, let us explain to them the situation at hand and ask if your spot could be held until January 2017. Then after that, if you feel that you still cannot attend, you can then decline. Would that suffice?

Mrs. Voltsclaw's response gave me excitement. Mom should be better by then. Dr. Agelwalabe stated that the treatment was a very advanced treatment she was receiving, and he's hoping for the best. I think that by January, Mom will be much better and able to travel with me; therefore, I respond back with: *Mrs. Voltsclaw, I agree. That gives me hope. I will contact them and see if that is an option. I will keep you updated. Thank you again.* I immediately pull my computer open and email the contact person. I tell her everything and request a hold on things until January. I hit send and hope for the best.

Mom is awake in her bed. She doesn't have the strength to get up on her own, so I go to her to help her sit up in her bed. Later today she'll have a nurse that will stop by. I don't understand why the doctors feel she needs a nurse when I'm going to be here, but I'll accept whatever help I can get so that Mom can get better.

"Good morning, Mom. Are you hungry?"

COFFEE

Mom turns toward me and says, "Good morning, sleepyhead. Yes, I am a little hungry, but would like my cup of coffee first."

Mom loves coffee. She drinks it every morning, and when I turned ten years of age, right before my brief illness, Mom started allowing me to drink coffee as well. It was like we had to have a cup of coffee together. She would watch me drink it, and if she wasn't around to make it, she made sure that it was ready. All I had to do was pour the water into my cup.

Mom asks me to bring the wheelchair over to her bed so that she could get into it. Mom is very independent. Even in her time of weakness, she likes to try to do things on her own. I push her wheelchair up to her bed and helped her get in, I then wheel her into the bathroom so that she can freshen up. I watch her as she takes her pajamas off. My heart is saddened because she looks so frail and thin. Just last week she had a little more weight on her, or so it appeared. But now it's like the weight is dropping rapidly. She slowly brushes her teeth; she spits into a brown oval-like container that we brought home with us from the hospital. We do this to minimize her having to constantly stand up to spit into the sink; however, every time she spits the toothpaste out, there is blood: more blood than I think should be there from simply brushing her teeth. She rinses her mouth, and I help her step into the shower. There is also a chair that the hospital gave us to place into the shower so that she can sit while showering. I turn the water on and adjust it just right. It was like the water was waking Mom up. She looks up and allows the water to flow onto her face and hair. She smiles at me; her strength seems to be returning. She washes herself and dries her hair. Then I help her get out of the shower, get dressed, and roll into the kitchen.

"What a beautiful morning today. Maybe we can sit out on the deck for a little while later. Would you like that?"

"Sure, as long as I have my cup of coffee with me, I would love that," she says. I'm watching her as she wheels herself over to the counter and grab her tea kettle. Mom would tell me that if she doesn't have her coffee in the morning, then she can't function. I've never been one to rely on anything to help me function but myself. The tea kettle whistles, and Mom grabs her favorite coffee mug and pours water into it. I immediately say, "No, Mom. You haven't put any coffee grounds into your mug yet."

Mom looks at me and says, "In all these years, you haven't noticed that I add my water first and my coffee grounds last? It's our family's way of making coffee: my mom taught me, her mom taught her, and so on. I've taught you, and in the future, you can teach your children."

COFFEE

I'm looking at her thinking, *She's right*. I *have* noticed that over the years, but it never stood out to me like it does now.

I respond and say, "Oh wow, you're right. Disgusting though, and you don't have to worry about me teaching my children at all because I don't like coffee." I give her a faint smile.

Mom turns toward me, looking appalled and takes her hand and provides a soft playful slap onto my backside, and says, "So what have you been doing while away in school, have you not been drinking the coffee that I send you?"

The look on her face quickly spoke volumes. It was obvious that if I was to say that I haven't been drinking coffee that she would be greatly disappointed; therefore, I lied. Yes, I lied to Mom, and I say to her.

"Yes, Mom. I've been drinking the coffee; I just don't make mine the way you make yours."

Mom turns completely toward me so that she can get a good look at me—or so that I can get a better view of the irritation that was setting in, and she says, "So how have you been making yours, Samantha Louise?"

The need to use my government name tells me that she is upset, and that trouble is on the horizon; therefore, I must shift the conversation. I surely don't want Mom upset right now. She needs as little stress as possible; therefore, I reach into my bag of "Mommie tricks" and say, "Oh, Mom, I'm just kidding. I drink the coffee exactly like you. No worries, ok?"

Mom takes the bait, turns back around, and says, "And don't be calling my coffee disgusting. You aren't too big for me to still whoop you."

We both find the humor and are amused at what she is saying so much that we laugh for quite a while. I finish scrambling Mom some eggs, and I place them on the dining room table for her to eat. I pick up her coffee mug and take it into the dining room while she's wheeling herself in as well.

"Mom, how are you feeling today?"

Mom doesn't immediately respond. She's busy with her coffee ritual of lifting the coffee mug and allowing the steam to permeate her nostrils. She holds her head back to get a strong smell of the coffee and lets out a moan indicating that the smell of the coffee was pleasing to her. Mom says that doing this opens her mind to allow a feeling of peace to overtake her before she begins her day. After she's done letting the aroma pervade her nostrils, she takes a sip and places the coffee back onto the table, looks up at me, and says, "I'm not good Sam, but I will be good."

"Mom, why didn't you tell me about your cancer?"

"I regret not telling you now. When I first found out, I was under the impression that it was a small

COFFEE

nodule on my lungs and that a few treatments would make things ok. I hadn't even had the treatments yet when I started getting sick again, I was throwing up blood constantly. When I would go to the bathroom to make a bowel movement, it was more blood than anything. After notifying Dr. Agelwalabe, he ran more tests, and came back and said that the cancer was all over my body. I was going to tell you when you were home this last time, but we were having such a great time, and I knew if I told you that I was going to start chemotherapy immediately, you would not have left for school, and I couldn't have my sickness causing you to drop out of college. I won't have it."

I continued staring at my mom. She's talking, and the whole time she's talking she hasn't picked up one fork of eggs, which she requested. But each time she takes a sip of her coffee, it takes her to a place of peace: her voice gets stronger, and she even looks stronger.

"Mom, you should have told me. I get what you don't want, but what about what *I* want? Do you know how terrified I was, getting that call from crazy Ms. P. and not knowing what was going on? You had just passed out on me before I left, and then this. I won't drop out of school, but I will take care of you. You raised me the best you could. You worked two jobs to care for me. Now it's my turn to care for you.

I'll stay here until you get stronger and better, young lady, so eat your eggs."

Mom, after hearing the authority in my voice, shakes her head in a sassy way as if to be mocking what I just said. She nods and finishes with another sip of her coffee. She takes a fork full of eggs, but while the eggs are in her mouth she begins to cough. The eggs fly across the table at me. I hop up, run to her, and pat her on the back.

She moves my hand away and says, "I'm fine, I'm fine. It's just swallowing anything with substance tends to choke me."

I look down into her lap to find the remnants of the eggs that she was eating, and they are covered with speckles of red blood. But I also noticed that right there in Mom's lap is a chunky substance, I take a napkin and use it to retrieve the substance from her lap, as I bring it closer to my eyes, I notice that this meat-like substance is not eggs: it looks like my mom is coughing up her *lungs*.

Is that even possible? I thought.

CHAPTER FIVE

Temple, TX
October 12, 2016

Mom's health is declining. She's on hospice now, and the doctors have said that things aren't going to get much better. She has stage four advanced lung cancer that has metastasized to other parts of her body, which are shutting her organs down rather rapidly. I can't believe what I am seeing. In this short amount of time, Mom has lost so much of weight. I feel helpless. This isn't supposed to happen this way. I lay in my makeshift bed that I have created in Mom's room. I pull the couch into her bedroom, and this is where I sleep now. I refuse to leave her side.

COFFEE

I jokingly say to her that we are now truly roommates; she nods in agreement. The weakness in her responding these days is evident. Her eyes are not as sharp anymore, the joy is no longer in her countenance…but I can tell she's fighting even though she's tired.

The morning arrives and it is beautifully bright outside, yet it's gloomy because I must care for my mom, whose cancer-ridden body takes my breath away. I'm awake and still tired; it's like I just laid my head down. I don't hear any birds chirping or the peaceful sounds that I like to hear these days. Nothing is soothing for me. I don't get much sleep anymore because I can hear her coughing in the middle of the night, and it scares me.

On top of that, now there is a nurse that has moved in with us to take care of Mom, Ms. Vernita C. Cox. She is a hospice nurse, and she's here every day and night. She has three children and no husband, but she has a live in babysitter that watches her kids. I guess that's needed when you have a family and a job such as this, but how can you stay away from your children? I'm sure it causes problems with them. She has been doing in-home hospice for seventeen years now, and she says that it brings her comfort knowing that she can help people in a time of need.

I recall when she and I had our first conversation, the peace that came through the words that she was saying were refreshing, but in the back of my mind, I understood her assignment: Ms. Cox is here because the doctors don't believe that Mom is going to get better. Ms. Cox has been so helpful in Mom's care and helping me fill out insurance paperwork that I wouldn't have known how to complete if she weren't here. I am shocked that Mom's insurance and financial papers were not already in order, but Ms. Cox said that when she looked at them, there were some discrepancies, so she volunteered to correct everything. Mom is usually anal about things of this nature, but I guess secretly dealing with this sickness has taken up much of her time. But Ms. Cox has been a lifesaver: she was able to get a temporary power of attorney form for me to fill out, which I haven't had time to complete. It was against my better judgement that Ms. Cox stayed here day-in and day-out, but now that she's here, I am grateful for her presence. She's such a sweet lady with an odd-looking tattoo on the back of her hand.

I sit up on my bed. Mom is awake.

"Hello, sleepyhead," she says, a name that she would call me when I was younger.

"What are you doing wide awake beautiful. How did you sleep?"

While Mom and I are talking, Ms. Cox comes into Mom's room with a tray. On the tray is all of Mom's medications, a small bowl of applesauce, a

COFFEE

small coffee pot that Ms. Cox bought her, Mom's favorite coffee mug, and a small bowl of the famous family coffee grounds. Ms. Cox administers Mom's medications to her. She then tries to get Mom to eat a little of the applesauce. Mom isn't having it. Instead, Mom looks over at me.

"Sam, have a cup of coffee with me," she says.

She knows that I don't drink coffee, so I reiterate.

"Mom, you know that—"

I stop what I was going to say because Ms. Cox gives me a look that a mother might give to a child as if to say, "drink the darn coffee."

"Ok, I will put some on for me," I said to her.

Mom shakes her head no, and she pours the hot water from her small coffee pot into her favorite coffee mug. She takes two spoons of the coffee grounds and dumps them on top of the hot water. I'm sitting on the side of her bed looking with utter disgust as these coffee grounds are floating on the top of the water. I can feel my throat thickening, and I want to gag, but I surely can't do that right now. Therefore, Mom begins to stir the coffee, and on her nightstand, Ms. Cox places the sugar cubes and milk. Mom points at it, and Ms. Cox hands it to her. She pours a drop of milk in, then takes two cubes of sugar and drops them into the cup. She's stirring slowly. I must admit that it does smell refreshing, but while Mom is stirring, her eyes are fixated on me the whole time.

"Drink," she says and hands her coffee mug over to me.

The remainder of that day was different for me. Mom sat in her bed, and I sat in a chair on the side of her bed. Her bedroom window was cracked slightly to allow the fresh air to come in. We could hear all the birds, horns, and the chitter-chatter that was taking place outside.

Mom keeps peering over at the window; therefore, I asked, "Mom, would you like to go sit outside?"

She smiles at me. She always had a wonderful smile. She nods but puts her hands on the top of her head to indicate that she wanted to cover her head. I had purchased Mom a few wigs, and she likes them, so I gather the wigs so that she can pick the one that she wants to wear.

I say to her, "Alright now, Ms. Lola. Which lady will you be today?"

Mom laughs, and she selects the wig that she wants to wear. She chooses the long wig; it comes past her shoulders and is very full. It's the one that came the closest to her natural look than any other.

Getting Mom dressed is not an easy task; therefore, Ms. Cox helps me get her dressed appropriately and into her wheelchair. We're about to go to the back to sit on the deck, but Mom says, "Let's go for a walk."

COFFEE

I'm happy to hear her saying that because Ms. Cox and I both had offered to take her for a stroll in her wheelchair, but she had refused. But today, she wants me to push her down the street, and I do. Ms. Cox helps get her out the door, and she goes back into the house.

The air on Mom's face is gracious to her. The wind is blowing like a whirlwind, but it isn't too much for her. There's just enough coolness in the air to keep her from becoming cold right away. She rolls, and I walk as we laugh and talk. We chat about so much like the good ole days and my dad leaving and how it was a blessing for us both. Things seem to be kicking in gear. Mom is happy, and so am I. How can I not be? At this point her happiness is what brightens my day.

When we arrive back at the house, Ms. Cox is sitting on the porch, waiting for us to return. She had cleaned the house, changed the bedding, vacuumed the floors, and washed the dishes. She also had filled out some paperwork for Mom, and all Mom had to do was sign the papers. The house smells so clean and fresh.

When we get Mom back into the house, I'm about to wheel her back into her bedroom, and she says, "Let's sit in the kitchen."

Sitting in the kitchen is something we do often because we have a huge bay window that overlooks the backyard onto the deck. Mom loves looking out of that window, even though there isn't much scenery out there. She loves sitting in the kitchen. We had a television installed years ago so that we could continue to eat and watch our favorite shows at the same time. This is what we loved to do.

I turn on the television, and *The Andy Griffith Show* is playing. Both of us love some Andy Griffith. She fancied Barney Fife, but I like the good ole Sheriff Andy Griffith. As she is sitting there watching and laughing at Barney Fife, I just watch my favorite girl. I appreciate her more than ever before, how she cared so much for me. Nothing else mattered to me now but getting her well. The hell with AU, the hell with Baylor. I will not leave this place until Mom is back to normal.

The tears begin to flow, and I slowly wipe them away to avoid her noticing that my heart is slowly breaking. I can look at Mom and tell that things aren't going well. I could see the sickness is invading her body fast making her precious private shell its new home. It was like a burglar is breaking into her home and is destroying everything in sight.

Yes, I have become emotional: very emotional. My head is on a swivel. I watch Mom, then the television…Mom, then the television…until Ms. Cox walks up behind me and places her hand on my shoulder, and whispers, "God be with you," into my ear.

COFFEE

She says to Mom, "Sharon, it's time to take your medication."

Mom looks up and nods in agreement. I can tell she's tired and wants to lie down; therefore, I tell her, "I'll be there in a minute Mom."

Mom has gotten to the point that she wants me around her as much as possible, and it sort of makes me feel good. Even though we have always been close, if my presence makes her feel better, then so be it. Mom lifts her left hand as if to say ok, and Ms. Cox wheels her away. Today was a good day, even amid everything.

Every morning when Ms. Cox brings Mom's tray into her room, Ms. Cox would have an extra mug filled with water and all the fixings. All I need to do is add the coffee grounds. Ms. Cox does this so that I can drink with Mom. Mom might hand me a spoonful of her coffee and direct me to stir my coffee. She prepares her cup, and we both drink the coffee together.

Oftentimes, Mom drinks out of the extra mug, and I use her favorite mug. I feel so special when that happens because Mom loves this mug. She'd never allowed me to drink even water from the mug when I was younger, but now she's sharing it with me. I don't push against it because I know this is bringing her joy. And I must say, the coffee is good. It had a distinct taste to it when I drink it from Mom's mug. Well, at least I think it does.

Apparently, the coffee originated from my great-great-grandfather who was a farmer. He grew coffee plants he acquired when his family migrated from Africa. He would harvest them to sell to the locals in the area, but when my great-great-grandfather became ill, he sold the farm to a local, who in turn, made a living out of making the coffee that Mom now drinks. Mom always would call a family friend to place an order for her to get the coffee in bulk. Mom would perform her ritual of blessing the coffee as soon as it would arrive, and she'd place it in the basement in what looked like a large pickle bucket. She said doing so would help the coffee maintain its freshness. Mom believed the new owner didn't know how to get the best out of the coffee. To him, it was just coffee grounds, but to Mom, it had a whole different purpose. To Mom, it had a healing component, and she was determined to maintain it, at least for her consumption.

The two of us follow Mom's coffee drinking routine every morning, and afterward we usually go outside for a stroll. Ms. Cox becomes more and more scarce: she's only here in Mom's room with me during medication time and to prepare our cups for Mom's coffee. Otherwise, she stays in the guestroom, out of sight. I reckon that's to allow me time with Mom alone. It's appreciated because the two of us are becoming closer than ever before. I didn't think that we could get any closer. Mom and I have a bond that was over-the-top. We're best friends, and the last few weeks have shown that we're one. She knows me better than I know myself, and I love every moment.

CHAPTER SIX

Temple, TX
October 18, 2016

The night is long, but I slept great, waking up feeling refreshed. As usual, I sit up on my makeshift bed and look over at Mom; however, usually Mom is up and awaiting me to open my puffy eyes. But this morning, Mom is still asleep.

I stand up, lean over, and kiss her on the forehead, deciding to take my shower first. I can hear Ms. Cox stirring around in the kitchen preparing to bring Mom her tray as she always does. I peek out into the hall, and Ms. Cox catches eyes with me. I mouth to her that I am going to take my shower

COFFEE

and that Mom is still asleep. She nods, showing her understanding and continues preparing Mom's tray. After I finish my shower, I come out, and Mom is already sitting in the wheelchair, waiting on us to take our morning stroll.

I say to her, "Well now, look who is bright and bushy-tailed and ready to roll."

She smiles, and I throw on my gray jogging pants with my gray Baylor T-shirt. It's a bit chilly—not cold—but chilly being that it's October, it could be colder. So, I throw on a jacket while Ms. Cox helps Mom into her coat and her wig.

She places a hat on Mom's head and jokingly says, "Alright now, be home by midnight."

Mom looks at me and says, "Let's roll, BFF."

The three of us laugh so hard at her because to hear Mom use any type of street slang is hilarious, and the funniest part was that she knew how to use it. Mom and I begin our normal routine, but there's something different this time. I don't know what it is; she's not talking much. I know the air is nippy, and I wonder if it could possibly be causing her a bit of difficulty with her breathing.

"Mom, are you ok? Is this air too much for you?"

Mom shakes her head no, and we continue our path. We go as far as we normally do, with me doing all the talking and her lifting her hand every now and then to signify agreement or disagreement.

After we reach our point of return for the walk, I turn her around and begin our quest headed back to the house. We are halfway there, and Mom puts her hand up to get my attention.

"Are you ok?" I ask.

She becks for me to lean down closer so that she could say something. I put my ear to her mouth, and she says, "Sing 'Jesus Loves the Little Children.'"

I'm surprised at her request because Mom and I aren't religious. We go to church every now and then, but we aren't every-Sunday churchgoers. I know the song, but I'm not a singer, so I give it the best that I can. I begin to sing, and Mom bobs her head every now and then. We finally make it back to the house, and Ms. Cox comes out to help me bring Mom inside. As usual, Mom wants to sit in the kitchen and watch television instead of going into her bedroom.

Ms. Cox is about to administer the second set of medications to her, when Mom stops her and points to her coffee mug. "Do you want coffee, Sharon?" Ms. Cox asks.

Mom nods her head yes, and Ms. Cox looks at her and then over at me. We're confused because Mom doesn't like to drink coffee during the day. She prefers it early in the morning and this would be considered late in the day to her.

Ms. Cox hands the mug to Mom as she puts the coffee pot of water on and begins to gather

COFFEE

everything that is needed for Mom's cup of coffee. While the water was getting hot, Mom was very quiet and serene. She sat in her chair waiting patiently, but I could see the anticipation on her face. I can tell there's something going on in Mom's mind. Her eyes are fixated in one direction, but her mind is elsewhere. The coffee pot finishes heating, and like clockwork, Mom tells Ms. Cox to pour the hot water into the cups. She then adds the coffee grounds and then adds the milk and sugar to her coffee. Mom stirs the coffee, and she takes her long whiff of smell, holding her head back as she takes in the bold aroma of the coffee. And she then takes a drink.

I'm standing in front of her, and Ms. Cox is on the side helping her hold the cup so that she won't drop it onto her lap. Mom then gestures for me to have a cup of coffee.

"No, Mom, I don't want any today," I say to her.

Mom looks at me and shakes her head yes. Ms. Cox gives me that stern look once again as she reaches over and retrieves a cup of coffee from the counter that she has already prepared and hands it to me. I reach over and take the coffee from Ms. Cox hand, but as soon as I was getting ready to take a sip, Mom throws her hand up to stop me. She then lifts her head to indicate that she wanted me to smell the coffee first.

"You want me to smell the coffee, Mom?"

She provides a gentle nod, saying yes.

I lifted the cup up to my nose and took a big whiff. The smell was more pungent than I recall it ever being. I held my head back as Mom would do, and at that moment it's as if I were taken up into the heavens. There's a peacefulness that overcomes me. My legs are light. I can't hear anything taking place around me. A warm feeling is draped within my body as I take a deep breath in and exhale. At some point I reckon the coffee mug is removed from my hand, and I continue in my few minutes of transition. I'm not sure how long my head is back, and my eyes closed, but what I do know is that during that time, nothing mattered to me. During that time I felt all would be ok, and it was during that time that I felt Ms. Cox's hand on my shoulder. When I open my eyes and lower my head, my eyes met with Ms. Cox's eyes. There's an air of vacancy that she personifies while attempting to bridle the tears that are beginning to pool. She looks at me with such sadness, drops her head just enough and directed it toward Mom.

At that moment it was almost like I knew what Ms. Cox was indirectly saying, but the peace that I have just experienced becomes a glove to the very being that I am. I take a deep breath, not prepared for the despair that is about to greet me. At that very moment, I feel empty, and don't know why until I look over at Mom. Her head is leaning back, her eyes

COFFEE

are closed, and her mouth is slightly ajar, just like when she smells her coffee.

At this point reality is making its way back. I can hear everything taking place. I can hear the television going. I can hear the noises outside. I can hear the car passing through the alleyway behind our home. My senses are heightened so much, and I realize that I'm no longer hearing any beeping from Mom's blood pressure machine. It's no longer getting a reading or a pulse from Mom. I look over at Ms. Cox, and she nods. I drop to my knees in front of Mom sitting in her wheelchair. I lift her hand into my hand and begin to rub the back of it. I take Mom's hand and place it on the side of my face and under my chin like she did on so many times to give me the assurance that I needed. I'm not sure as to how long I sat in front of her like that. I don't think I would have moved if I hadn't heard Ms. Cox moving around. I stand up and begin to remove all the medical devices that are attached to her. I straighten her up properly into her chair. I fix her wig and her clothes. I walk over to the television and turn the channel to *The Andy Griffith Show*, which just happened to be ending. As the tears begin to flow from my eyes, I kiss her on the forehead, pull a chair from the kitchen table, and place it directly beside Mom's wheelchair. I sit down beside her and lie my head onto her shoulder and say, "Good night, my favorite lady.

CHAPTER SEVEN

Temple, TX
November 16, 2016

I have a peace about Mom's death. It's as if she and I made up for the time missed while I was away at college. I was angry for a moment because I didn't truly understand why she hadn't told me earlier about her sickness. But after talking with her doctor and the oncologist, they helped me understand that when Mom found out that she had cancer, she was already in stage four. There was nothing much that could be done other than keeping her comfortable and hoping for the best, and they did just that.

COFFEE

It takes me a while to get in touch with all the family and friends. Everyone is very helpful—even Ms. P., once she got over herself. The day Mom passed, I call Ms. P. to inform her, and she comes running into the house, falling onto the floor screaming, "Sharon, oh Lord, my Sharon. Come back, Sharon. Come back."

It's sort of comical. Ms. Cox looks over at me, and I shrug my shoulders and say, "This is who she is."

We both give a chuckle and allow her to get it out of her system. Once she's done, she stands up and gives proper condolences, asking what I need her to do.

The homegoing services are beautiful. Mom is dressed in her favorite colors: pink and white. On top of her casket is a huge, beautiful spray of white roses with pink carnations mixed in between them. There's a white ribbon hanging down from the side of the flower bouquet. In gold writing on the side, it says, *Loving mother*.

There are so many people. Many of my high school and college friends came to show their support. I sit on the front row alongside my aunts and uncle, watching Mom's friends view her beautiful remains that laid so still. Many walked up and extended their condolences to me. I had no idea of who they were; maybe at some point I did but not today.

My mind seems to be slipping away from me and I seem to be having a hard time recognizing everyone. The many church ladies who come up and hug me leaving their strong perfume scent on me. I'm sure by now I smell like a cheap version of a department store's perfume aisle.

Oh, how I despise walking past the perfume aisle in Sears. The perfume ladies—that's what I call them—never seem to take no for an answer. They walk up to you and ask if you wanted to try their perfume, and before you have a chance to say no, the spray of their strong-smelling liquid quickly becomes air droplets that—regardless of how fast you moved or how you tried to avoid it—it manages to attach to your clothing for the remainder of the day. I would begin to cough and wave my hand to minimize myself breathing in this bouquet-scented tear gas and choking the remainder of the walk through the store.

Today was not one of my favorite times, but on this day, the day I am mourning my mother, I'm feeling like I want to take off running every time I see one of those ladies approach me. I'm in a church, but all of this brings back those memories.

I get a surprise because Ms. P. informed me that Mom had started going to church every Sunday after I left for college. Mom had a church home for two years and never told me. I guess she was allowing me to discover God on my own.

COFFEE

Ms. P. introduces me to Mom's pastor, and I meet Pastor Joshua Arnold III of the Blessed Hope Baptist Church. Pastor Arnold is a little bit older than Mom; he's a handsome man with no wife or children. He had become the Pastor only a year prior to Mom joining. After seeing him, I'm sure Mom's new walk with Christ had something to do with her "blessed" hopes of getting closer to this man, like all the other single women in this church. Pastor Arnold is prior military as well as a big gym rat. He has broad shoulders, a bald head, and is clean shaven. He carries himself with confidence and speaks with a voice that's assuring…or should I say alluring?

When Mom's good friend, my Aunt Robin, arrives she immediately asks who Pastor Arnold was, and of course, Ms. P. makes it her business to take Aunt Robin over to meet him. She also gives her the 411, 911, resumé, and analysis of Pastor Arnold. I think Ms. P. may have wanted him for herself, but she knows deep down that even trying to date a man of such caliber as Pastor Arnold is out of her league. So, she conceded, living vicariously in hoping and wanting those that she knew would make the mad dash in their attempt in getting a chance with him.

Also, Mrs. Voltsclaw attended the services. I truly appreciate that. And before she leaves, she tells me to reach out to her when I can, and I oblige.

It appears anyone and everyone that Mom ever knew attended her services. I'm overwhelmed with the "Hello, thank you for coming," and the fake smile that seems to have affixed itself to my face. Even when I want to cry aloud, I can't muster up the tears to get them to drizzle down my face. I'm frozen with a smile, and I'm ok with doing so at first because I know Mom would have wanted it this way, but I'm tired. I want to go home, and I am so done with all of this.

The time comes for them to close Mom's casket, and I don't want to go back to view her body again. My heart is pounding. My mouth is feeling like it's stuffed with cotton balls. I feel dehydrated, but Aunt Robin insisted. What she doesn't know is, I'm having a bit of anxiety looking over at Mom lying there. But Aunt Robin grabs my hand, and we walk slowly toward the casket. The closer I get, the faster my heart begins to pound and the drier my mouth becomes and the more it appears as though Mom doesn't look like herself.

I let go of Aunt Robin's hand to place my hand on the side of the casket. I recall mumbling something, but the words wouldn't come out of my mouth. Was I trying to scream? What was I trying to say? Why won't my mouth open? Am I crying? I'm here at the casket, but I don't see Mom. The only thing I can recall from that moment is that I could hear Aunt Robin and Ms.

COFFEE

P. calling my name and tapping me on the side of my face. I'm trying to open my eyes, and all I could think is, *Where am I, and what's going on?*

GROUND ZERO

I am here, it doesn't feel right without Mom. I must admit that I'm still angry. How could Mom just leave me? How could she not have fought harder so that I wouldn't have to endure being alone?

I'm feeling overwhelmed, and I realize that Mom's death has taken a toll on me. I'm waiting for the hospital to come and get the wheelchair, shower chair, and the hospital bed that she refused to sleep in. They don't wait too long to say they need to pick these items back up.

The driver finally arrives, and they take everything out and load it onto their van. I sign the paper, stating that everything was returned, and I watch them pull away. Ms. Cox has come to the house to have me sign some final papers. I'm glad she came because she was able to get a large order of Mom's special coffee for me. She made sure that everything I needed was taken care of, but she had to leave. And now I'm here alone in this house, which has an eerie feeling.

No Mom and no Ms. Cox.

The emptiness of the house awakens the hollow feeling within me. I'm plunged into an inner abyss with no way out. It's so quiet that I can hear a pin drop or a mouse sauntering across the floor. My head is spinning. My temperament is mercurial, and I'm feeling isolated. I decide to go into Mom's bedroom to lie across her bed. I can still feel her presence, and I can still smell her despite the smell of medication and disinfectants that Ms. Cox constantly used. Surprisingly to me, none of that was able to distort Mom's redolent perfume, leaving me to feel as if Mom was still here.

I can't bring myself to say she's dead because Mom being dead isn't resonating within me. No, I'm not in denial as others suggest I might be. I understand all about grief, but this isn't the same. I can't help but feel that Mom isn't gone; she can't be. I ask myself, *Right, Sam?*

As I lay in her bed, my head begins pounding, and my mind suddenly begins to race. I don't want to be here anymore. I don't want to be alone. My heart is beating fast. This is worse than when I was at Mom's funeral. I feel like I can't breathe. I want it to stop, but the tears won't stop. Am I having an anxiety attack? What's going on?

I take the pillow from Mom's bed, and I place it over my head, *This won't work, Sam.* I turn over onto

COFFEE

my stomach and bury my face into the pillow. *Mom, come back and get me.* Why didn't she take me with her? My mind is playing tricks on me, I believe I can hear Mom downstairs walking around. I'm trying to gather my thoughts, but I can't. I need to get it together. I'm just tired and need to rest.

I get up from Mom's bed and go into her bathroom. I'm looking at myself in the mirror, and I say over and over, "I don't want to do this. I can't do this." But I must.

My head is hurting, and I need to rest. So much has transpired within a few days, and I've only had three hours of sleep. My whole world has been turned upside down. I'm seeing things and hearing things, and I just can't do it anymore; therefore, I open the medicine cabinet, and I find an unopened bottle of belsomra sleeping pills. I hold the bottle in my hand and look into the mirror at myself. My mind is speaking to me in a language that I am not familiar with,

"*Take the pills and sleep it all away*" is what I am hearing,

"No, Sam. What are you saying?"

It's just pills. You need to get away from it all. Take the pills, and you won't have to worry about any of this again. Go ahead: one big handful.

I feel like I'm in a battle within myself. I'm hearing things. I'm so angry, not just with Mom, but with the nurses from the hospital. Ms. Cox, Dr. Agelwalabe...everyone that met with Mom and didn't help her. I'm even mad at Ms. P. How does she get to live, and Mom doesn't? She's annoying, and no one likes her. It should've been her. I'm angry, and someone needs to take responsibility for Mom getting sick so fast and dying.

Yes, I need to rest; therefore, I pop the lid and fill the cup that is sitting on the sink with water. I pour the pills into my hand and drink the cup of water. The tears are stronger now and are making their way down my face and onto my shirt. My vision is blurred because of the amount of tears that have accumulated. I stumble my way back to Mom's bed. This is the first time that I have cried this hard. If this is grief, then my level of grief is beyond what I imagined it would be. My best friend is gone, and I hate my life. As I lay there, I begin to hear all sorts of noises around me: doors closing, people talking, telephones ringing.

Get it together, Sam. You are ok. You are ok.

I close my eyes and take a deep breath and I slowly exhale. I recall Mom use to have me take a deep breath and exhale slowly when I would get nervous and excited. Therefore, I go through these steps once more, but this time as I inhale, I don't smell the disinfectants, nor do I smell Mom. What I smell is the aroma of Mom's coffee. It's as if Mom is in the

COFFEE

kitchen at this very moment making herself a cup. I take a deep breath in, and I allow the coffee smell to take me away, but this time, I'm going farther than I've ever been before. I can hear a whispering within my head talking to me. What am I trying to say? My eyes are heavy, but my body is feeling light. My lips are moving, but nothing is coming out.

Oh no, Sam. I think you've gone too far because where I am now is ground zero.

CHAPTER EIGHT

Homestead MI
November 23, 2016

Whew! I made it! I've learned so much from the time I arrived here. I can't believe how quickly things has started to shape up for me since being here. I'm sitting in a café window on this beautiful crisp morning, reading and drinking a cup of Mom's special coffee that I bring with me here to the café. As I look outside the window, I see an elderly woman struggling with a few bags. Her back is a bit bent over. I reckon she suffers from osteoporosis or scoliosis. I watch her as she walks past the café window. She stops at

COFFEE

the door and comes in. She orders a cup of coffee, but she doesn't have enough money. I overhear the barista tell her that the price has changed, she sighs and looks all through her pockets. It was then that I got up, walked over, and handed the barista the difference when another woman comes from out of nowhere and stands beside the elderly woman just looking at the two of us. She reminds me of Ms. P, being so nosey and finding her way to know what is always going on with anyone and everyone. I walk back over to where I was sitting in the window booth to finish reading my book.

"Hello, young lady. That was such a nice thing for you to do," says the nosey lady.

"Oh, not a problem, I had the same problem the first time I realized that the prices had changed; it was the barista who helped me." I'm saying this and looking around to see if the other lady had sat down, but she was nowhere in sight.

"Do you mind?" the nosey lady says nodding her head at the booth that I am sitting in.

"Oh, not at all," I say while moving my bags around to the side that I am sitting on so that she could comfortably sit on the opposite side.

"My name is Eevi," she says as she stretches her hand out to shake mine.

I extend my hand to her and say, "I'm Samantha, but people call me Sam."

"American, are we?"

"Yes, I'm American."

"Such a beautiful place, you know. I've visited America a few times."

"Oh, really? Where at, may I ask?"

She's sipping her coffee, and responds with, "oh no place in particular, all over, I reckon."

Watching and listening to her talk, I don't hear the Swedish or Finnish accent that most of the people here carry, so I ask, "Are you from here?"

"Where exactly is 'here' these days?" she asks reticently.

"Here in Finland," I say to her. "I've been in Finland since January."

Eevi smiles with an awkward and a mischievous chuckle and says, "Truth is, I'm not sure where I'm from." She asks, "So, you just arrive to Finland this year?" Then she stands up and gathers her things, saying, "I must be on my way. Enjoy, my dearie."

Oddly enough, no one calls me that but Sonny. *Too funny*, I'm thinking as I watch her walk down the street.

Time is passing, and I've become bombarded with trying to create a design for an upcoming competition that will take place on campus. The winner will have the opportunity to work alongside a famous designer and possibly have their own design featured. The director is looking for a particular type of dress. He wants a Victorian-style dress with a rustic look, but it must have the early nineteenth century overtone to it. This is competitive; therefore, others are creating the same dress, and Vaughn Conley, one of the school's design directors, will judge which dress best suits the look he's requesting. Getting my design chosen would be huge for me, so I'm taking a lot of time preparing this dress in hopes of it getting chosen. I have six more days to finish and submit. Oh, how I hope my dress is chosen. I'm very nervous because others have said that Vaughn is very harsh. Although, he doesn't look harsh…he appears a bit soft. I guess he's what many say have the hard-boiled egg appearance: hard on the outside but soft on the inside. Truth is, I'm scared of him. I'm scared that he'll think that my design is trash. But he's well connected, so I must take a chance. I can hear Mom saying, "You got this. Make sure you dot every *i* and cross every *t*, and if he doesn't pick you, then it's not for me."

November 29, 2016

Submission day is here, and I've spent countless hours working on my design. I arrive at the auditorium, and as I walk in, I notice that all the designers are assembled, maybe adding last-minute touches. Some are so confident that last-minute touches are of no concern to them. They're just standing beside their design that's perfectly affixed to a headless mannequin or professional dress form. These designers are fabulous; the work that I'm seeing is beyond amateur. I see professional-looking designs that are amazing…and intimidating at the same time.

I'm thinking, *Maybe I shouldn't be here. Am I out of my league? My designs will never stand up against these designers. What was I thinking?* Then I can hear Mom in my ear: "You deserve to be here like any other designer."

I snap out of my beginning stage of having a personal pity party, and I proceed into the auditorium. There will be three rounds, we were told, and if you are lucky enough to have Vaughn choose you in the first round, you will move to the next round. It's then when the design for round two will be announced and when we are told what would be expected.

Vaughn begins to walk up and down, up, and down looking at all the dresses that are assembled. He's made it clear that he will only pick fifteen designers to move to the next round. He points to someone and says, "You." He walks to another, points, and says, "You."

He's walking toward me, and I'm thinking, *He's coming my way. Get ready, Sam.*

COFFEE

I take a deep breath, he looks my way, and walks right past my design without even looking at it. I exhale, and my heart drops. He continues to walk but he then takes a step back, stops, point, and says, "You," but to the guy who he had walked pass that is two dresses to my right.

He continues to walk, and I'm taking a mental count of how many dresses he's chosen thus far. He's already at thirteen, and my design hasn't been chosen. I can feel the tension rising in me. The sweat is cascading down my back. I'm nervous and can feel my heart pounding louder than ever. Vaughn is making another round when he walks toward me again, but this time, he's looking at my dress. Once again he passes right by me and chooses the designer standing directly next to me. "You," he says, and I'm thinking, *Nooo, pick me. Pick me, you were supposed to pick me. That was fourteen, and there's only one spot left. Please, pick me.* I swallow as the tears are bubbling up like a backed-up sewer system. A knot is beginning to form within my throat. I'm starting to concede—to accept that I didn't get chosen. I watch as Vaughn stands on the other side of the auditorium. I want to run out of here to avoid the inevitable embarrassment that is sure to come, but I stand strong, and there it is: the knot has formed in my throat. I want to cry so bad; I worked hard to get here…to design this dress. I can feel my head slipping down, and suddenly from across the room I hear, "And you."

I look up to see who he had chosen, and Vaughn Conley is pointing his black and gold pointer stick directly at me. Shocked and unsure, I put my hand on my chest as if to say to Vaughn, "Me?"

"Yes, you," he says.

I don't know what to do. I stand more erect and confident, but that one tear decides that it wanted to be defiant; therefore, it breaks loose and takes its path down the side of my face. *Hold it together, Sam. You got this. Never let them see you sweat.*

I discreetly take the side of my jacket, lift my shoulder up, and wipe the tear away before anyone notices it. I proudly gather my things and take the walk of excitement back to my home. The tears of joy are doing the happy dance on my face; nothing seems to matter to me at this time. I must celebrate, but with whom? I don't know anyone. I arrive home and sit down on my couch. I want to call my mom and share the good news with her. I wish so much for her to know that I had been chosen in the first round, but there is no Mom to celebrate with. She's gone, never to return. There are no friends, so I celebrate internally and alone. My heart hurts, so I lay down, and I fall asleep.

CHAPTER NINE

The Auditorium

It's Tuesday, and I'm drinking coffee. Meeting Eevi in the café has become a part of my weekly routine. I am excited to share my good news with her. I walk into the café and wave at Olson the barista who never says much. Olson waves back as I go over to my normal booth in the corner and await Eevi, who should be arriving soon. I look out the window and notice that she's crossing the street—very timely, she is. I give her a slight wave as she enters the café and goes up to the counter. She retrieves her cup of coffee and comes over to sit in our booth.

Eevi says, "Hello there, how are you today?"

COFFEE

"I'm ok. I've been very busy; I'm involved in a dress designing competition that has me a bit nervous and stressed."

"Sounds very interesting. Would you like to talk about it?"

Eevi is so loving and patient. I don't know much about her, but she seems to be interested in what I'm doing, and I want to share the stress that I am dealing with right now. Maybe talking it out with Eevi will help me relax a little; therefore, I say, "I guess… it's just…I'm going up against a lot of fabulous designers, and I barely made it through round one. I was the last person he picked, so it makes me think that my design wasn't so great if I was his last choice."

"Oh, dear heart, don't think like that. I'm sure your work is as good as any other. From what you've told me, you were invited to compete in Finland. Therefore, you have a gift. Don't compare yourself to any designer, especially not the Finland designers, because you are just as great as they think they are." Eevi is saying this as she reaches over and touches my hand.

The touch of her hand on mine sends chills down my spine. It has a nurturing feeling, like a mother would touch a child, as if assuring the child that everything would be ok. I thought about moving my hand, but I allow it to remain and embrace the motherly warmth.

"Thank you, Eevi," I say as she and I continue to sit and chat about everything that we could think of. After more than an hour had passed, I say to Eevi, "Well, I guess I'd better be on my way. Will I see you next week?"

Eevi stands up grabbing her bags and says, "*Pistää mehiläinen,*" which means "do a bee sting" in Finnish, and she walks away. Eevi is a fast walker, and by the time I grab my bags and look out the window, she's gone. She's out of sight and on to folly in her daily activities, as she puts it.

I pack my stuff and head over to the auditorium for the reveal of the type of design we would need to create for round two. As I walk into the building, Vaughn is standing near his office door with his back turned to me, talking with several of the other designers. The conversation appears to be going well with them. Many of them are familiar with Vaughn and have attended several of his seminars. I'm the newcomer on the block and don't know anyone; therefore, I walk over to where they're standing so that I could become acquainted with them.

As I approached, Vaughn looks back over his shoulder and proceeds to walk into his office. The remaining individuals dispersed into different directions. It's at that moment that I knew my presence isn't welcome. For me to succeed in this game, I'm going to have to step it up.

COFFEE

Vaughn comes out of his office clapping his hands saying, "Gather around people, gather around."

Everyone drops what they were doing and rushes to the center of the floor. I put my bags down and start walking in his direction. I must admit, I don't rush as everyone else did; I don't sense the urgency that it appears that my fellow cohorts did. So I took my time, unfortunately, to Vaughn. My doing so was a blatant level of disrespect to him, and so he commences to verbalizing his displeasure for my actions or inactions by saying, "Darling, I don't know what is up your hinder parts, but whatever it is, you better get it out now. Because when I say 'gather around,' I mean gather around, and that doesn't mean for you to take your sweet, little time, so get over here now!"

I want to ask him who he thinks he is, but I can't. I must pace myself. I must adjust to their culture over here just like I adjusted to Ms. Voltsclaw and her culture. I can adjust here. I immediately put a little pep in my step and hurry over to where everyone else had gathered, and I offer my apologies.

"Thank you for participating," says Vaughn with a condescending look on his face.

He begins to tell us what is expected for the second round of designs. All the other designers are ecstatic about what Vaughn has chosen, but when I heard the words that were coming out of his mouth, I nearly passed out right where I stood. Vaughn goes on to tell us that for round two, we are to create a menswear design, but it must combine traditional wool with great knitwear texture. The design must host patterns that marry swashbuckling shapes with an Elizabethan court and rubber stamp–style print. He expresses that any design void of these requirements would be immediately dismissed.

Vaughn asks if anyone has any questions. I *so* wanted to raise my hand to ask what the hell was he talking about. I'm not familiar with the terminology that he's using, but out of fear of being openly reprimanded or humiliated, I keep my mouth shut and listen closely to the other designers as they discuss the task at hand. By listening, I quickly learn that what Vaughn had chosen was pretty much the everyday attire that one would see here in this chilly town of Helsinki.

CHAPTER TEN

The Encounter

Walking around Helsinki helps me in understanding the fabric of Finland. I take notice of everything and everyone around me. I pay close attention to everyone's movements, and I pay even closer attention to the way they're dressed.

I see people with Elizabethan-style clothing. I see people with jackets that are knit and textured, but what I *don't* see is anyone with the swashbuckling style of clothing that Vaughn is requesting.

Upon arriving at my apartment, I go in and decide to do something that I don't normally do: I

COFFEE

decide to make a cup of coffee in the middle of the day. I can't believe that I drink coffee every day now, but it must be exactly the way Mom makes it, or I won't drink it at all.

I reach in my bag and grab Mom's special coffee mug, I pour the boiling hot water in Mom's coffee mug, and just like Mom, I add two scoops of coffee directly into the water and begin to stir. I sit down at my counter and take a big sniff of the coffee and hold my head back, just like Mom. I remember the last time that I had a good cup of coffee like this was the day Mom passed away. Things have never been the same for me. I'm still angry that Mom isn't here. I'm still angry that she didn't tell me about her sickness. I'm still angry that we didn't get a chance to spend more time together. I'm still angry, and yet I want to forgive her.

I must forgive: forgiveness is for me, not for her. My mind is all over the place. I need to think. I can feel myself becoming overwhelmed; therefore, I decide to go down to the café to get some fresh air and to free my mind.

I arrive at the café, and no one is at the counter. I don't see Olson, so I go right over to my normal booth and sit down to drink my cup of coffee. *Mom, oh Mom, I didn't get a chance to tell you that I would be coming here to Helsinki, Finland. Oh, how I miss you.* The tears begin to flow from my eyes.

As I look out the window, I notice Eevi briskly walking across the street. I don't catch her attention because at this moment I just want to be alone to think. I put my head down into my arms onto the table and sob.

"Hello, young lady. Fine to see you here," says a voice standing over me.

I lift my head up, and my eyes connect with Eevi, who was standing directly over me. She smiles at me and proceeds to sit down.

"What's wrong? Are you ok?"

"Hi, Eevi. Yes, I'm ok. I'm just thinking about a few things...just want to be alone right now."

Eevi looks at me, takes both of her hands, and slaps them together making a loud clapping sound. She says in a very authoritative tone, "Snap out of it. Whatever it is that's bothering you, you must get over it. Nothing shall control you."

Shocked from the loud clap of her hands and even more shocked at the tone that she was using, I say to her, "Eevi, I'm missing my mom right now, and it's getting the best of me."

"Oh, honey, I get it, but there is nothing you can do about your mom. She's gone and not coming back. Now get over it. Let's enjoy the moment."

I sit back into my seat in total disgust, shaking my head from side to side because now I'm angry with Eevi. I say to her, "How dare you attempt to

COFFEE

downplay my feelings? How dare you? I can't enjoy the moment, Eevi; I'm hurting. I'm a bit stressed, I don't have a mom, and I really need her right now."

Eevi is laughing, and I'm taking offense that she has found humor in my sorrow and stress. The sound of her laughter, the look in her eyes, and her body language are offensive enough to anger me.

She stands up, places both hands palm down on the table and says to me, "I'm your mom now. You have a mom."

I don't respond right away. I'm dumbfounded at what's coming out of her mouth, and I'm furious at her behavior. I stand up and shout at her saying, "You're not my mom, and you can never be. Get the hell away from me!"

Eevi jumps up from the table, looks at me, flips me the bird, and walks away. The amount of anger that is permeating my body right now isn't healthy. I don't ever recall feeling this type of anger with anyone before. I'm so angry that I want to punch her in the mouth, grab her by the back of her head, and slam her face down onto the coffee table. Yes, that would release a lot of my stress; therefore, I grab my coffee mug, and I storm out of the café with steam coming from my ears, and I go looking for Eevi.

CHAPTER ELEVEN

The Designer's Place

Time has gotten away from me; I'm almost two hours late to the designers' work area. Vaughn has established a space for the designers to work on their projects undisturbed. I begin to walk toward the Flamingo Hall, the location that Vaughn has set up. Vaughn has it such that only four designers at a time can be there: each person is allowed up to four hours each day.

Upon my arrival, I see four areas sectioned off that remind me of office cubicles. Our names are affixed above the areas that we're assigned to. Each area has partitions all around them, separating everyone.

COFFEE

I guess this was done so that the designs are kept private and so that no one could distract each other. To my left, I see the name *Herschel Pinto*; to his left was *Elea Koski*; to her left, I see my name: *Samantha Scott*. This is where I'll be working for the next four hours. I smile and lift my chest in honor when I see my name. Proud I was, and proud I am, and to my left is Tomás Guerra. When I see Tomás's name, I get a childlike giggly feeling within me. Tomás is from Portugal. He is very cool to talk to; however, it's not Tomás that makes me behave like a schoolkid…it's knowing that Tomás is roommates with my new love.

CJ, this young man has stolen my heart and attention. Oh gosh, he is handsome. CJ stands about 6'1, maybe 6'2, with broad shoulders and a strong chest. He wears T-shirts all the time, which advertise his muscular biceps and accent his rock-hard triceps. He has long brown hair that is locked on the top, usually in a ponytail, and he keeps the sides cut short. His dark color and deep voice grab the attention of everyone when he walks into a room, mainly because he's so dark, but also because it's obvious that CJ is an American from Newark, New Jersey. He's here because he plays semiprofessional rugby and could go pro. Oh, how terrible it is that I'm so attracted to this CJ…this man that I really don't know. The only thing that I know about him is that he's friends with Tomás, who will soon be my new BFF.

In my cubicle I begin to lay out some of the ideas for my men's design. I'm setting up everything, and in walks Vaughn. Following behind him is a young lady named Jax. No one calls her by her full name because no one can pronounce it. Jax reminds me of one of the nurses that helped Mom while she was in the hospital.

I recall one day the nurse came into Mom's hospital room, and I told her that Mom was in a lot of pain and needed more medication. She responded with, "Oh ok, but she just had a dose, so she can't get another for an hour."

I looked at her and said, "Are you serious? She's in pain."

The nurse then replies, "What do you want me to do? I can only administer what I am told to administer."

I became so irritated that I jumped up and walked out the door. I was standing outside waiting for her to come out so that I could give her a piece of my mind, but just when she walked out, Aunt Robin was calling. I needed to take the call, and I got over it. But every time I see Jax, she brings back those bad memories that I have of that nurse.

Jax is always under Vaughn. If I didn't know any better, I would think that the two of them were an item, but after watching and listening to Vaughn talk about his life and lifestyle, I realized that Vaughn is

COFFEE

under no circumstances interested in a female and surely not one that is named Jax.

I peek over my cubicle to see where he is going, and he's making his rounds to everyone's area. I immediately pull more items out of my bag and arrange them onto the worktable to appear that I have been here for a while, but in walks Vaughn with a vexatious look on his face.

He says to me, "So I guess you're so great of a designer that you didn't need four hours?"

"Oh, no it's not that, I had an important errand to run before coming here."

Jax is standing at the entryway to my cubicle as Vaughn walks around lifting the items from my table inspecting them. He says, "What's so important that you didn't show up for this session? This session is critical for everyone, even you."

"I just had errands—"

"Yes, you've said that, and I've asked you what was so important."

I'm totally stunned by his emotions. I look over at Jax, and she's standing there with a smug look on her face.

I stop what I was doing, and I reply with, "Vaughn, with all due respect, what I had to do is of none of your business."

Vaughn looks back at Jax and the two of them begin to laugh. He turns away from me and says,

"Touché." He then writes something down on the clipboard that he carries around with him. Vaughn is always coming in and out of the cubicles daily, asking questions and taking notes. As he was about to walk away, I thought that his daily visit was over, but Vaughn turns back toward me and says, "I just pray that before you start working on anything, you clean those filthy hands of yours and get that dirt off your clothes. Nobody wants to see a dirty design."

Vaughn and Jax are slowly walking outside my cubicle, and I can hear them whispering as they walk away.

Jax says to Vaughn, "I can tell that Ms. Sam is still confused; she has a long way to go."

Vaughn replies, "Oh honey, I've seen worse that come along, and they end up bouncing back. Never underestimate anyone."

I look over the top of my cubicle, and I can see Jax reaching into her pocket. I notice that she's showing Vaughn a small book…a book that resembles my planner that I had sitting on my table.

Jax tells Vaughn, "Look at what I have."

"What is it?" he says.

"It's her planner. I took it from the table while we were in there."

Vaughn is seemingly annoyed at what Jax has done, and he says, "Why did you take her stuff? Take it back."

COFFEE

Jax is laughing as if she were watching a comedy show while flipping through the pages of my journal. She says, "I will, it will show back up in her possession after I go through it."

Vaughn is clearly not in agreement with her behavior and says to her, "You are so immature Jax. Your behavior is the reason why you are suspended. Now give it back."

"I will Vaughn, lighten up, in due time," says Jax, as they walk out of the building.

I'm beyond furious. All kinds of thoughts are running through my mind, *She stole from me. What kind of place is this? What kind of people are they? Why am I being tested? First Eevi, now this darn warlock Vaughn and his witch of a sidekick, Jax.* I pick up my coffee mug, take a huge sip thinking, *Well, they have the wrong one. I'm not who they think I am. I'm going to get my book back now.* Standing at my table in such anger, I look down at my hands and my clothing. I begin thinking, *How did I get so dirty? And where did this dirt come from? I need to clean myself up…what a mess, Sam.*"

CHAPTER TWELVE

Aalto University

I arrive at class and notice that the atmosphere appears to be a bit gloomy. I go and sit down at my seat. I begin taking my books out of my bag in preparation for class when I overhear the whispers of two ladies standing over to my left side. The one in the green-and-blue plaid sweater says, "Hey, did you receive that text from Alpha?"

"Alpha, the secretary's son? No, what text," replies the one lady who is very tall and pale.

She's so pale that her skin tone is like a ghost. Her hair is in a punk rock mohawk style with a hot pink color to it. The one in the green-and-blue

COFFEE

sweater walks closer to her and says, "See, this text about Jax."

Jax? Upon hearing that name, I begin to listen more intensively. I'm thinking, *What about her? What do they know about Jax?* I take my eyeglasses out of my bag and place them onto my face. Mom always said, my glasses won't help my hearing, and I know it's crazy, but for me, it does.

No, I didn't get that text. Where is she? Does anyone know?"

"No, all it says is that her family states that she never came home."

"She's always with Vaughn," says the pink haired girl. "I wonder if he knows?"

The girl in the sweater just shakes her head, and she walks over toward me to take her seat. When she sits down, I want to ask her what it was that she was saying about Jax, but I have yet to get to know anyone. And so far, the folks I've met don't seem friendly.

As class gets started, one of the administrators comes to the door and becks for the instructor, Mrs. Amelia Arnett. Mrs. Arnett is one of the many design instructors here in Aalto University. I have her for two different classes. She is warmhearted, mild mannered, and quiet. She's not brash or aggressive, but she is strict: a stickler when it comes to submitting your work. She told us at the beginning of the semester not to take her kindness for weakness. She stressed that if you do the work, you will have her undivided attention and help within this class. However, if you do not do the work, your behavior tells her that you aren't interested in passing, and from there she will not extend herself to help you. Others grumbled and mumbled at her comment, but I found it to be refreshing.

Ms. Arnett steps out of class with the administrator, and the two of them are in the hall conversating. The plaid sweater–wearing girl says out loud, "I wonder if that is about Jax."

"Shut up, Elly. You don't know what they are discussing," says one of the males from the back of the class.

Just then, the door to the classroom opens and Mrs. Arnett walks back in, she stands behind her desk and picks her cell phone up and scrolls through her text. From the look that is on her face, it appears that maybe she has received a text informing her about Jax as well.

Mrs. Arnett places her phone back onto her desk and says, "Class, before we get started, I don't know how many of you are aware, but there is a text from the family of Jekaatariinna Koskinen, whom everyone knows as Jax. Her family is seeking information because Jax hasn't been seen in two days. The family is asking that if anyone knows her whereabouts or

COFFEE

knows anything, to please notify the school or the family."

It's at that time that Mrs. Arnett writes two telephone numbers on the chalkboard.

The mumbling begins immediately. Everyone has their own ideas of where she could be, and none of the ideas overlap.

Some say, "She's with her boyfriend."

Others say, "She's with her girlfriend."

Even more say, "She's probably somewhere hungover."

Just then, the outpour of assumptions takes the backstage when the pink-haired girl says, "They better check Vaughn."

Upon hearing Vaughn's name, someone says, "Yeah, I saw the two of them a few days ago coming from the designer's place. They were arguing about something, and whatever it was, Vaughn was not happy about it. I bet he's hit her before."

At the sound of hearing that Vaughn could have hit Jax before, the class erupts in loud conversation.

One says, "Vaughn hit Jax?"

Another says, "Well, I haven't seen him hit her… just shove her. But I did see her and someone walking over by that café. They were walking toward the woods. It looked like they were arguing."

As the chatter grows louder and the accusations become more boisterous, Mrs. Arnett turns around and says, "Ok, ok, that's enough, everyone. Someone is missing, and we don't know why. Please refrain from all the assumptions concerning her whereabouts. If you know anything, notify anyone here, even the school."

Everyone begins to laugh when the pink-haired girl says, "The school last, Mrs. Arnett? Why did you mention them last?"

Several students chime in: "Yes, why the school last? And why did you make that face when you mention the school?"

Mrs. Arnett says, "Settle down. Call whomever you like, no preference here. Now, let's open with our daily affirmations."

The loud chatter comes to a halt, but directly behind me in a small whisper, I heard a voice say, "Because of Mr. Mosley."

CHAPTER THIRTEEN

The Café

I'm sitting in the café, and I must admit that the time alone for me is working out for my good. I'm sitting here, perusing my design ideas, and taking a moment here and there to peer out of the window. I'm reminded of how, at this time, Eevi usually crosses the street. Eevi is a very prompt individual; by now she should be walking through the door… but no Eevi.

I continue making changes to my designs when a female walks up to me and says, "Hello, my name is Fina. Can I get you something?"

COFFEE

Thrown off a bit by her appearance, I look up at Fina standing there. She looks as if she could be Ms. Cox's daughter or sister. The only difference is that Fina is a pale-looking young woman with tattoos on her neck and arms. She has very short black hair—it's evident that dye was used to create such a look. Her nails are painted black, her lipstick is black, and even her eyebrows were jet black. The ring in her tongue is a huge distraction for me, but even with all of that, there's something in her eyes that reminds me of Ms. Cox. And before I could even respond to her, my thoughts were loud within my head thinking, *I didn't know that Finnish people were also Gothic.*

I turn toward her, and I respond with, "Oh no, thank you. I usually just bring my coffee and come over and sit down."

Fina gave me a strange look and says, "Ma'am, we don't allow people to just linger; we have a strict policy. This space is usually reserved for sessions; therefore, if someone has reserved the space and you are waiting on them, please let me know.

A shocked look came across my face when she made the statement "reserved the space." I respond with: "Are you serious, since when?" I go on to say, "I've been coming here every Tuesday at this time for a few months, and not one time did Olson make me order anything. Can you tell me when did this rule you are speaking of went into effect?"

Fina sighs and says, "There is nothing that went into effect; this has always been our rule. And today is Wednesday. So again, unless you have reserved this space, you will have to leave. I can give you a cup of coffee to take with you."

"No, I don't drink 'your' coffee; I bring my own. This is crazy. Where is Olson? He'll tell you."

"Ma'am, I'm here for the day, please go."

"Is Olson here?" I ask.

By this time, I'm becoming very irritated, and my voice has risen to an abnormal octave for me. I don't sound like myself. I'm wondering if my dark complexion or strong tone is scaring her or throwing her off. I don't want to accuse her of being racist, but she's not being helpful. She's rude, and she's trying to make me place an order. I've never had to do that before, and I refuse to do it now.

Fina says to me, "You must leave." She's noticing the irritation that I'm now exhibiting, so she then walks away.

I'm not sure if she's walking away to go get Olson or what, but at this point, my anger is ahead of me. Therefore, I grab my stuff and hurriedly walk toward the door. I look over toward the counter, and I can see Fina in the back with the phone in her hand. I imagine she's calling Olson or the manager, either doesn't matter. Calling Olson would be better for me: he'll be able to clear this up.

COFFEE

I then say, "I'm leaving, but I'll be back next Tuesday, and tell Olson I'll talk with him at that time."

Fina shrugs her shoulders and says, "Whatever."

I walk over to the auditorium, and the door is closed, which is unusual because someone is always inside. As I walk up, I see a note affixed to the door that reads, *Everyone please meet me in the main hall for an announcement.* The note is signed, *Mr. J. C. Mosley.*

I'm thinking, *The famous Mr. Mosley…I'll finally get a chance to meet him.*

I turn around and stroll over to the main hall. One of Mom's biggest pet peeves with me was that she would always say that I found no need to hurry for anything. She would jokingly comment that the house would be ablaze before I'd realize that I needed to get out.

I arrive over at the main hall; all the designers are there, standing around and whispering.

I can hear them chattering with the same questions that I had: "What is this about?" and "Where is Vaughn?"

In walks a tall Frankenstein-looking man. His silver hair was all over his head, but oddly, he has a long black beard and black eyebrows. He wore thick glasses, and his voice was so deep and intense that it makes the room appear to rumble. I'm sure he never needs a microphone when speaking to a crowd of people. He appears disheveled in my opinion, but what do I know? I've never set eyes on him before so this could be his normal appearance.

Everyone stands silently, and in walk several other students. To my excitement, Tomás was among them, and right behind him was my knight in shining armor, CJ. I wave at Tomás to get his attention in hopes that he and CJ would come stand near me, and as I had hoped, Tomás and CJ both come over to where I'm standing. But following behind CJ is another black girl.

"Hey there, Sam, how's it going? You remember my roommate, CJ, don't you? Oh, and this is Lolita."

I know I must have appeared to be dumb and stupid because for a moment I stood there with my eyes transfixed by CJ. *He's so fine. I love him, but she—this Lolita—she's, she's…oh my, she's gorgeous!*

Then Tomás said, "Hello, Earth to Sam. Are you ok?"

I extend my hand to CJ, and I almost melt when his hand touches mine. *Stick your tongue back in your mouth, Sam. Get a grip, girl. You got this.* And I respond with, "Yes, yes, CJ, how are you? Good seeing you again." I look at Lolita, but I can't figure out the right words to say—I can't be mean, I must be cordial—so I blurt out, "Hi."

And then I turn my attention toward Mr. Mosley, thinking, *Oh no, she has to go."*

COFFEE

Mr. Mosley is fidgeting around. I can see why everyone says he's odd. He places his fingers in his rear beltloops as he's pacing back and forth. He then lifts them both and says in a very loud voice, "Attention, students. Jax has been found, but she's dead. They found her body in the woods over in a dirt pile: her face had been bashed in, and Vaughn is upset so he told me to tell you all."

He says this with no compassion, turns around, and walks out of the building. He left everyone standing there trying to grasp what we were just told, feeling heartbroken, upset, and needless to say: scared. So many of the girls are crying. A few of the guys are comforting some of them. Some of the guys are in shock, and some of them are crying as well.

One of the students says, "This is horrible. Who would do that to Jax? She was such a nice person."

And as I'm listening to them and their foolishness, I'm thinking, *Bull. She was mean, sneaky, and she couldn't be trusted. She got what she deserved.*

Tomás looks over to CJ and says, "I wonder what happened. And what does this mean for the competition?"

"This is some wild stuff going on, bro. I can't believe she's been killed…not just dead, but she's been *killed.*"

CJ is saying this while he's comforting Lolita with his hand around her shoulders. I could just walk over to her and snap her spine into two. I really wished she would stop pushing up on my man. The nerve of her.

One of the students loudly says, "It was Vaughn. I told you I've seen him and her fighting before. It was him."

Then another student chimes in saying, "I haven't seen him hit her, but the way they would argue…I wouldn't be surprised. Besides, where has *he* disappeared to?"

As everyone proceeds to walk out of the building, I see a figure in my peripheral vision. The figure is moving between the two buildings where there's a small nook that leads to nothing. As I turn my head to get a clear view, I notice Mr. Mosley peering sneakily at everyone walking out. When he realizes that I see him, he steps back into the nook and slips out of sight.

CHAPTER FOURTEEN

The Apartment

I'm lying on my back across my bed while my eyes appear to become one with the ceiling. Here in Finland it's more daunting than I ever imagined. Back home danger was never this close. In retrospect, I don't ever recall feeling like I was in danger. I could walk the streets at all times of the day and never feel like anything would happen to me. I don't know, maybe I'm overreacting; I can't say. However, I do wonder if high crime is a common thing around here.

I must admit, after seeing Mr. Mosley, the comments from Mrs. Arnett and the students about him

COFFEE

are a bit concerning: he *is* a pretty creepy dude. The excitement from today has my thoughts all over the place. I guess I'm becoming addicted because I decide to get a cup of Mom's coffee and relax my mind. Today has been a long day.

I make my coffee, take me a long whiff of the aroma, and hold my head back. I thought drinking the coffee would relax me and put me to sleep, but instead, it was like a jolt. And now I cannot sleep. I want to walk down to the café. Maybe Fina and I got off to a bad start. I realize that she was just doing her job, and her questions were innocuous. I will go there tomorrow, apologize, sit quietly, and oh yeah, place an order.

It's Tuesday morning, and I arrive at the Café like normal, but to my surprise and pleasure, there is Olson. He's busy with something. I want to talk with him concerning Fina—not to cause conflict but to get a better understanding—so I go over to my booth and sit down as usual. I'm sitting there looking out of the window; the nighttime here in Finland is a beautiful sight. The air is just above freezing—crispy, I might add, but it is something that I'll have to get used to. I'm still adjusting to the long days with no real dark nights, and I'm waiting to see a true sunset. I've been told that to see a typical Finnish sunset, I'll have to wait until late November, but it's beyond that time, so I guess I'll wait to see a sunrise, which I was told would happen around mid-January. I'm not sure what is meant by "typical," but right now here in Helsinki, I am experiencing around fifteen hours of daylight.

I'm sitting in the booth, and I have yet to see Fina working around. My guess is that she and Olson never work on the same day. I sit patiently waiting on Olson to return to his station, but it appears that won't happen.

I can't believe that Jax is dead and that Vaughn is a suspect. I don't believe there was a romantic relationship between the two, but I could be wrong. Vaughn is controlling, arrogant, and can be a bit pushy, to say the least. What could possibly be the reason for him and Jax to disagree about? Could it be something connected to designing?

I realize that because Vaughn is not around at the time, the competition could possibly be on hold. But if I'm correct, if Vaughn resurfaces, he's going to want to pick up right where he left off with the competition, and he's going to expect us all to be prepared. Tomorrow I'll walk over to the library so I can research the culture here a little further. I'm starting to realize that every day here in Finland is really a different day: never take it as ordinary.

I'm gazing out of the window, and there she is: Fina. She's across the way, walking toward my apartment complex. I hurry up, grab my bag, and run after her.

COFFEE

"Fina, Fina," I'm calling behind her.

Fina turns around to see me, but she continues to walk. I finally catch up with her and stop her just as she turns down the side corridor near the dumpsters. It's dark, but I still need to apologize to her.

"Hi Fina, I just wanted to—"

Fina is standing directly in front of me and interrupts me by saying all sorts of insulting things. I try to stop her; there's a significant amount of anger building up in me.

Yet, I say, "Fina, I'm trying to apologize."

As I'm saying this, my head begins to spin. I begin to envision me pushing her back further into this corridor and hitting her across the head with that pole that's sitting over in the corner. I bet then she wouldn't be so disrespectful. I'm staring at her for a while, then my phone rings. I look down at it, and when I look up, Fina is no longer standing in front of me.

CHAPTER FIFTEEN

The Library

I wake up, and I'm feeling a bit refreshed. I prepare myself a cup of coffee. Yes, coffee. I take my usual whiff and hold my head back. As much as I'm fighting against this sudden urge to drink coffee in the mornings, I think this is going to become a daily ritual for me. I'm finding myself depending on it. Mom would be surprised just at the thought of me drinking one cup, but she'd be even more surprised that I'm drinking it more than expected.

I put on my clothes, grab my parka, and head out the door. I recall when I first arrived here, I was told that the area that I was living in was a very poshed

COFFEE

area, particularly for the tourists that come into town. Therefore, I ask the *kellopeli*, or bellhop, the directions to the library. I'm walking and taking in the sights, and I arrive in front of this huge building with many steps. Several individuals that I assume are tourists are standing around taking pictures of it.

This building is beautiful. It's all white, and it has five green domes. It reminds me of the Islamic buildings one would see back in the States. It appears to be a fairly new construction. I take out my cell phone and begin to snap pictures just like the others, and I overhear one of the tourists talking to a small child standing to his right. I can't tell if the child is a boy or a girl because the child's hood is pulled so tightly on their head that I cannot get a clear look. The tourist tells the child that this is the Helsinki Cathedral, and that it's one of the most impressive landmarks here in Helsinki.

He says, "If you look up you can see the statues of the twelve apostles decorating its rooftop."

The child looks up and says, "*Näen, näen*," which translates to "I see, I see."

My Finnish is not that great, but I'm learning a few words, and for what I don't know, my handy-dandy iPhone is the best tutor.

I arrive at the library, and what a library it is. This library is *huge*; it's Helsinki's central library. I'm not positive, but I recall hearing that this library was chosen to somehow be symbolic of the relationship between the government and the population.

This library is carefully organized. It has an open-plan reading room on the upper floor, which is named "book heaven." There is a café, restaurant, and I believe it houses a movie theatre as well. I'll find out for sure eventually. For now, I am a bit overwhelmed with its structure and I don't know where to look.

Everyone in here is walking around as if they are on another planet. The upper surface of the library is a canopy structure where people can stand and look directly over the square to the main entrance of the Finnish parliament. I have yet to see a librarian. I stop one of the many people standing around and ask where to find books on the culture of Finland. Rudely, the individual just points and walks away, but I'm directed to this large section of books. It's there where I find what I am looking for.

I grab the books of my choosing and take a seat in one of the overly spacious reading rooms. I begin to research the culture, and before I know it, it's three hours later, and I need to get back. I have a little over an hour before I must be at the auditorium. I gather up all the books that I was utilizing and replace them back on their proper shelves. I have taken numerous snapshots of the pictures within the books, and I've taken countless notes. I believe that I have what I

COFFEE

need to fulfill the intimidating task that Vaughn has assigned to us.

On my walk back over to my apartment, I walk through the cultural district. I peer into some of the windows and just walk by many others. But as I peer into this one window, I see an individual that appears to look like Vaughn. I stop to get a better view, and when the individual turns to his left side, I can make him out; I know that it's Vaughn. I'm sure of it because of the earring in his left ear. I stand in the window, waving and trying to get his attention but to no avail. Someone has his attention, though, because he waves and smiles at whomever it is that he sees from afar, and he walks in that direction.

I decide to go in. I open the huge, double glass doors and walk in. I then realize that this is a jewelry store that I'm standing in. I love jewelry, but I'm on a mission, and I have no time to stop at the many counters to shop. I see Vaughn walking away, and ahead of him is a male. He has on sunglasses, a blue-green baseball cap, a green T-shirt, and black jeans; his style of dressing is more American than Finnish. His hands are in his pants pockets, and his shoulders are hunched up into his neck. It appears that he's trying to be incognito.

I continue to follow Vaughn as he gets closer to the male waiting on him. It's then that I notice that the person Vaughn is meeting with is in a disguise.

Vaughn and the male approach one another and embrace with a kiss and Vaughn rushes him out of the back door of the jewelry store. I'm not shocked that Vaughn is kissing a male, I'm just wondering why he hasn't reported back to the school so that they can get to the bottom of what has happened to Jax.

I continue to follow behind—but not too closely—as the two walk hastily out of the door, down this dimly lit corridor, and around a left turn. I arrive just in time to see Vaughn and his inconspicuous friend going into this large black door.

I walk up to the door, twist the knob, and it's locked. I can't get in, but I can hear talking on the other side; it sounds like there are three different voices. I can make out that one of the voices is Vaughn's, but then there are two other voices: one is another male, but the other voice is not. The other voice is a female, and this female's voice sounds very familiar.

CHAPTER SIXTEEN

The Corridor

I awake to the sounds of police sirens and loud talking. The feeling of having a very active night of drinking and partying engulfs me. I slept very well; I had not partied nor had anything to drink. I can't imagine why my body feels so tired and sleepy. I can hear walking and talking in my hall, but just when I'm about to walk over to place my ear against the door to hear better, I notice that there's a piece of paper that has been shoved under my door.

I bend down to open it but immediately became distracted by the sudden brash banging on my door. It startled me such that I jumped back and dropped the piece of paper. The knock continues, but this time it's accompanied with the sound of the voice of someone who identifies himself as the Helsinki *poliisi*.

"*Poliisi, poliisi*, open," is what is said on the other side of the door.

Out of panic, I run to my bedroom.

"Poliisi, open now!"

I quickly pull my joggers on, grab a T-shirt, and I say, "Coming, one second," in hopes of providing me some time to gather myself. I quickly walk to the door, and as I open it, I'm greeted by a brutely built individual that addresses me with no care or concern in the world.

"Are you Samantha Scott?"

"Yes, I'm Samantha Scott. Who wants to know?"

"Ms. Scott, we have questions concerning the murder of Natasha Tounee. We found her body beside the dumpster behind this apartment, and we need to ask you some questions."

I give him what I'm sure is a look of confusion. I'm still feeling hung over—from what and why, I have yet to figure out. My hair is in disarray, and morning breath is present. And the witches have chosen to ride up and down my face, leaving their white skid marks near the creases of my mouth and the corners of my eyes, clearly showing that my face needs a good washing.

"Who? I don't know that person. I'm not going anywhere."

"Ma'am, you can make this easy or hard. We shall wait."

"For what? I don't know her?" I say this while slowly attempting to close my apartment door.

The officer puts his foot in between to keep me from closing the door and says, "Ma'am, don't make this hard on yourself. We just have questions. Come with us, and we will determine if you know her or not."

I stand there for a second and ask, "What is the name again?"

"Natasha Tounee," the officer says to me in a strong-but-evident Finnish-English accent.

"No, I don't recall that name. Should I?"

The officer lifts a photo up to me and pokes it closer to my face than I would have liked. I step back so that I can gather a better look. The photo is of a female that's lying face down near a huge, blue trash bin. She's wearing a black shirt and black jeans. She wore only one black boot with a white stripe on the side of it. Her other foot was totally naked and twisted in the opposite direction; surely it was broken. Her right arm was bent behind her back, palm up, but I can slightly see the black fingernail polish on one of her nails and a few tattoos on her arm. Her left arm is under her lifeless body, and there is what

COFFEE

appears to be some kind of pole resting on her back from I guess what was used to kill her.

"I'm not going to ask you again. Please come with us," the officer says to me with a very jarring tone.

I respond quickly, "No, I don't know her, and I don't think that I've ever seen her. Sir, I'm new to the area, and I'm not coming to the station without a warrant. I know you all do warrants here in Finland, right?"

He removes the photo and places it in his pocket. He then hands me a card and says, "If there is any information that you can provide, or if you recall hearing anything, don't hesitate to call me." He goes to walk away but turns back toward me and says, "You have a piece of paper on your floor."

He bends down to pick it up and I immediately grab it before he does, and I say, "Yes, I'm aware. Thank you." And I slowly close the door.

I'm in total shock. A young woman is dead, right here where I live. I'm terrified, scared, and in awe that I'm living in such an area. What is really going on? And I question myself whether coming here was a good idea. I then open the piece of paper; it's a handwritten note that says, *I saw you, and I know you saw me. Meet me at the corridor at 10:30 today.* It's signed with the letter *V.*, could that be Vaughn? He's the only person that I know that has a name that starts with that letter, and I *had* seen Vaughn.

Could this be from him? He still hasn't been back to the school. I look over at the clock, and the time is 9:17 a.m. It's still early. How was he able to get into my building? And how long has this note been here?

I arrive to the corridor early. I see no one; therefore, I go and stand near the tree. Standing over here provides me with a better view of when someone enters the corridor. I continuously look behind me just in case the person comes from behind. I turn back around, and I can see a person walking toward me, but I can't make out who it is. But as I turn back toward the corridor, I'm startled when I see Vaughn standing on the other side of the corridor with a gray hoodie pulled up over his head. He's wearing a baseball cap, his hands are in his pockets, and he's staring at me. When he realizes that I've made him, he turns to walk away and gestures with his head for me to follow him.

I'm following behind him as best as I can, but he's moving quickly as he turns down this court way into this dreary corner that I've never noticed before—it's creepy. I'm hesitant to follow, thinking, *What if Vaughn killed Jax and the lady that was found near the trash bin behind my apartment? What if he now wants to kill me?*

So as I approach the court way, I stop and I say to him, "I'm not going any further. I don't know what's going on. Why did you want to meet with me?"

COFFEE

As Vaughn turns around, he looks as if he is on his last leg. He's extremely tired, and it appears as if he hasn't had a meal for a few days. I feel very uncomfortable talking to him, and I'm just about to say that to him when—from out of the darker area of the court way—I see movement.

I quickly turn to walk away, and I hear my name called, "Samantha."

I turn back around and standing right in the corner of this dreary court way, right behind Vaughn is none other than Jax. She's standing there in black joggers and an oversized black sweatshirt.

"Jax!" I exclaimed. "You're dead. They've found your body!"

"*Shhh*. I know, I know, but that wasn't me, I'll… well…we'll explain later, but for now we need your help. Please help us."

Confused by what I'm hearing and seeing, I say to her, "*Me?* How can *I* be of help? And I don't know either of you well enough to help you do anything."

Vaughn interrupts and says, "Exactly, which is why we came to you. You haven't been here long enough, and people don't know you, so you can help us investigate what's going on. Someone tried to kill Jax, but it wasn't her. That was her *roommate* who was wearing her clothes; they look alike. They bashed her face in, Samantha, and once it gets out that it wasn't Jax, they're going to come after her."

Startled at what was just said to me, I look at Vaughn and say, "What's with you Vaughn? Why haven't you returned to the school? Everyone's looking for you. And why is someone after you all? I'm not getting into any mess with either of you. Call the police, they'll help."

"Don't make the mistake that I made, Samantha. Someone came to me for help, and I refused, and now I'm the target. Besides, we can't trust the police."

"What? That doesn't make sense. You're a target because you refused to help someone? That's ridiculous. And why can't you trust the police? No, no, I can't take part in this."

Vaughn steps up closer to me. He then says in a very convincing voice, "You want to win the designer competition, don't you?"

"Of course, I do!"

"Well, it would be in your best interest to help us. Helping us will help seal the deal for you." He says this looking lugubriously at me. I've never seen Vaughn show such weakness before. He must really need help.

Therefore, against my better judgement, I say, "What is it that you need me to do?"

Vaughn becomes soothed and palliated, he then says, "We will notify you. Just know, Samantha, that you cannot tell anyone that you've seen us…or what we're doing, do you understand?"

"Yes, I understand. When will I hear from you again? And what's the deal with the competition? Can you give me some insight now so that I can start working on my design?"

Vaughn suddenly ducks down and looks past me suspiciously as if he sees someone coming. As I look back to see who or what he was looking at, I turn back around to get his answer, and Vaughn and Jax are nowhere in sight.

CHAPTER SEVENTEEN

Danger Awaits

I rush back to my apartment, but now the yellow police tape is wrapped around the building like some sort of Christmas bow. The residents are instructed to see the officer standing at the door, and we must provide identification to verify that we reside within the building. I walk up to the officer and present my identification. He lifts the yellow tape and, without saying a word, he gestures for me to enter.

Walking up the stairs to my apartment I'm feeling shaken, confused, and still very tired. As I open the door and walk in, there's another piece of paper that has been slid under my door. I pick up the paper, and written on it are the words, "*YOU ARE IN DANGER.*" There is no signature like the earlier note, and I don't recognize the handwriting.

I quickly close my door, I'm feeling afraid, I go into each room in my apartment and close all my blinds. I sit and ask myself, *What have you gotten yourself into, Sam? Should I just go to the police with everything?*

I gather my bags in preparation of getting to the auditorium by 2:00 p.m., and I head over to the coffee shop. I arrive at the coffee shop and walk in. To my surprise, Olson is standing at the counter helping someone. I stand in line for my turn, and as I approach the counter, Olson rudely walks away as if he hadn't seen me. I stand there a little longer, then decide to go over to my normal area to have a seat.

The thoughts that are running through my mind are overwhelming. Vaughn and Jax are into something dangerous, and now they have pulled me into the same thing. Again, I'm wondering if I should just call the police and notify them of what Vaughn and Jax said. I take out my canister that contains the coffee that I had prepared at home, and I take a few sips. Surprisingly, the coffee is still hot. I'm sipping and drinking, deep in thought of my next move. I can't even think about designing anything right now. I'm a nervous wreck, and my mind is all over the place. I take another sip, and as I look up, I see Eevi coming toward the coffee shop.

I'm a bit excited to see her. I could use her to vent to, and I can apologize for my behavior a while back. I noticed Eevi walking this way, but she didn't come into the coffee shop, so I jumped up and ran to the door and opened it to greet her, but she's nowhere in sight. This doesn't make sense. I just saw her coming this way; therefore, I step out enough to see if she had gone into any of the other establishments along the way. But she's nowhere to be found.

I walk back in. Olson is standing there, looking in my direction. Surely he had to see Eevi through the window. I walk up to the counter, and I go to address Olson, and my phone dings.

I look down at it, and it's a text from Vaughn. I look back up to address Olson, and he's gone, and I think, *Can this day get any better?*

I decide to walk over to the auditorium early, and as I arrive, I notice Mr. Mosley in Vaughn's office going through some of his papers. I walk up and say, "Hello, Mr. Mosley."

Apparently my presence startled him because he jumps, and all the papers that he was holding fell to the floor.

His irritation with me becomes evident as he says in a very brash tone, "It's not two o'clock, why are you here?"

COFFEE

"I was over at the coffee shop and decided to just check in early. Is that ok?"

Quickly walking away from me, Mr. Mosley says, "Stay out of my way."

I'm so confused and really don't understand. It appears that no one likes me. I don't care. I'm not here to be friends; I'm here to win the spot as the top designer. I begin to set up my workstation, and once again I get a text on my phone. I look down at it, and I don't recognize the number. I assume it's either Vaughn or Jax because it says, *Tonight at eight behind the auditorium. Don't be late.*

As I was getting ready to respond, everyone started walking into the auditorium, and Mr. Mosley comes out and prepares to address us.

"Everyone, your next event requires a costume; it must represent a dark figure of crime."

As usual, when the next design is announced, the students all begin to mumble in confusion.

From over in the corner someone says, "A dark figure? What does that mean?"

Another student says, "I'm confused. Your instructions aren't clear."

Mr. Mosley looks over at him, lifts his chest to display his air of authority, and says, "What did you say, sir?"

The student chuckles slightly and says, "I said your instructions aren't clear. You just said a 'dark figure,' and we don't know what a dark figure is."

Mr. Mosley stares at the student that I have now realize is Herschel Pinto, one of the top designing students here at the school. It's said that he is a sure-in to win the competition. Apparently, Herschel has won many other competitions, and his resume boasts accolades from prestigious individuals. It's said that he once received a letter of recommendation from Mr. Jake Van'Iskar, a well-known dress designer around Europe: a savant, many would call him.

Herschel continues to laugh and poke fun at Mr. Mosley's request, and the other students begin to chime in and laugh, making mockery of the requirement.

"Shut up, all of you! Just shut up, you foolish students. Think! Use your creative minds if you even have them. This is the requirement, and it's expected to be done in three weeks…no, *two* weeks, since you all are so smart. Have this done and back to me in two weeks, and let's see if you will be laughing when you are cut from the competition, you morons." Mr. Mosley says this, swiftly walks out of the auditorium, and disappears.

No one knows where he's gone to; he's left all of us standing there, wondering. Mr. Mosley has an office in the school, but the door is always locked, and

COFFEE

no one ever sees him go in or out of it. If a meeting with him is requested, he always tells the student to meet him in the auditorium. Now, Mr. Mosley is gone, and I have questions. My only hope is that Vaughn is serious about helping me if I help him. I shall see tonight at 8:00 p.m.

CHAPTER EIGHTEEN

The Secret Meeting

I'm a bit nervous and I'm still not sure as to who the note is from. As I'm approaching the auditorium, I notice flashing lights from around the back. I pick up my pace, and as I step around the back, I see the countless police officers standing and talking. The lights from their cars are so bright that it blinds me. I lift my hand to make a shield over my eyes, and I notice the same officer that knocked on my door coming toward me.

He says, "Samantha Scott, right?"

"Yes, that's me. What's going on?"

COFFEE

"What are you doing out here at this time of night? It's late."

Feeling a bit taken aback from what is going on, I take a long pause before answering...long enough that he says, "Hello, are you ok?"

"Sorry. Yes, I'm ok. I was going for a walk; that's it, a walk."

He looks back over at the scene where the officers are and says, "Going for a walk, alone, at this time of the night? Do you think that is a good idea? We're getting more of these situations than normal."

As he goes to walk away, I call out, "Sir, sir, what's going on? And what are 'these situations' that you're talking about?"

The officer turns back around toward me and says, "Situations like this: finding bodies. We've found another dead body."

"Another female body, oh no!" I exclaim. "That's horrible!"

"No, no, not a female this time. This time we've found a young male."

The officer walks away and leaves me standing there alone to figure out what is going on. I begin walking back to my apartment; I'm rushing because I'm not sure if Vaughn or Jax has done this. What are the odds that a male's body is found in the area that I was supposed to meet them?

I walk in and take my jacket off. I sit there quietly for a moment, trying to take in what's happening all around me. I look at my phone to see if Vaughn has texted. Maybe he went to meet me and saw the chaos as well and aborted the meeting. Maybe he was there but couldn't meet with me because of what he and Jax are caught up in.

I go to call his phone, but I'm immediately hit with, *No, wait. What if Vaughn's body is the male body that they've found?* I drop my phone and exhale back onto the couch.

I must have dozed off because I'm awakened to my phone ringing. It stopped, and I pick it up. I look down at it, and apparently, I had slept for over an hour. The time is now 10:13 p.m.

Ring, ring, ring. There it is again. I look at it, and it's the unknown number that texted me earlier, but it's calling me this time. I'm hesitant to answer, but on the last ring again, I pick up and I say, "Hello."

"Hi Samantha, how are you?"

"Hello, who is this?"

With a chuckle, the person on the other end says, "Don't sound so disgusted, it's me, CJ."

"CJ, hi, how did you get my number?"

"What do you mean?"

"As I said, how did you get my number?"

"Everyone's phone numbers are posted on the electronic portal of the school. I'm sorry; I got your number and wanted to talk to you. Was this a mistake?"

I should've been excited to hear from him because I do like him, but so much is going on and I'm confused as to why CJ would text me to meet him at the auditorium instead of calling me. I move the phone away from my ear and look at the phone number again to verify it was from him.

I say, "No, not at all. It wasn't a mistake, but did you text me earlier today?"

"No, I think texting is so impersonal for the first encounter, so that's why I just called. It seems like this is a bad time. Maybe another time? Is it ok for me to call you tomorrow?"

I really, really like CJ, but I don't know what's going on. So instead of telling him that I know it was him who texted me, I say, "I'm ok, what's going on?"

CJ and I talk until well after two in the morning. We discuss the upcoming design that Mr. Mosley has requested, and we discuss being back in the States. We discuss each other, but we *don't* discuss the earlier text, and surely, I don't talk with him about Vaughn and Jax. It feels so good just to have a good conversation with someone whom I totally understand…someone who's a full-blown American. CJ. Yes, my new friend, CJ.

I finally get my eight hours of sleep. I'll work on my next project a little later, I'll spend the most of today getting more acclimated to my new life here. I walk into the kitchen to make myself a cup of coffee, and as I pass by my front door there is, once again, another note.

I'm thinking, *Come on now. Just leave me alone. I'm tired, and I'm not sure this is a good idea.*

I pick up the note, and it's from the officer. I guess he had been here, and I didn't hear him knocking, so he put a note up under my door. The note says, *Ms. Scott, please give me a call, I have questions about the body that we found.* It was signed *Officer Mendro*.

I dial this Officer Mendro, and he immediately answers. "Halloo, Ms. Scott. I've uhhhhh been waiting to hear from you. Thank you for calling."

"No problem, but how did you know it was me, and when did you come to my house to leave the note?"

Laughing, he says, "Everyone here has caller ID that shows the number, don't you? Anyway, I left the note around 1:00 a.m. I didn't knock because the time was not good, and it was late. I just put the note under your door."

I'm listening to what he's saying, but I'm also thinking, *I was up to well past 2:00 a.m., and I don't recall seeing a note on my floor at the door. Surely, I would have noticed it. That doesn't make any sense.*

Therefore, I say, "Interesting, what can I help you with? I've already told you that I don't know any Natasha whatever-her-last-name-is."

"No, I don't want to discuss Ms. Fina from the other day, I want to discuss the male who was found yesterday. When can I see you?"

"Oh, the male. You never told me anything about him, and I'm sure I don't know him either… and did you say, Ms. Fina? I thought the lady's name was Natasha."

"Well, yes. Her name is Natasha Tounee. She went by the name of Fina, but Ms. Scott, I beg to differ about you not knowing either of them, the male in particular. When we found his body, he had a bookbag with him, and in that bag was a planner. As I looked through the planner, I noticed that it appeared to belong to you. Ms. Scott, do you own a planner?"

"A planner? Yes, I own a planner."

"Can you describe it for me?"

"Well, it's black with a white stripe across the top, and my name and info on the inside. It's one that I can use over and over. Why?"

"So, how did it get in his bag?"

"I don't know, …wait, I just remembered; it was stolen last month."

"Stolen? Do you know from where and by whom?"

"Yes, it was stolen by Jax, one of the students from the university."

Office Mendro sighs and says, "Jax, the young student that was found bashed to death?"

"Yes, that's her. She stole it last month, and I never got it back."

"Why would she want your planner?"

Listening to Officer Mendro and the way he's posing his questions, I pick up that he's not believing my story, so I begin to be careful with my words because I'm still not sure as to what is going on with Vaughn and Jax, and too many dead bodies are suddenly popping up.

I say to Officer Mendro, "I looked at it as a silly joke. She was trying to play a trick on the new girl, no big deal."

"Samantha, we will figure the planner out later, but can you come to the station to talk to me today? I have something I want to show you and discuss with you. Who knows? You may be of some help to our investigation."

I'm feeling irritated. My plans were to stay home and just get my apartment organized. I have yet to put things where they need to be, and now I'm the one who's sighing.

I respond with, "Yes, I guess. I'll be there in an hour."

"Thank you so much. We won't keep you long. See you soon."

CHAPTER NINETEEN

The Police Station

Arriving at the police station was interesting. Unlike back in the States, there isn't a walk-up desk where you would find a heavyset police officer sitting, drinking coffee, reading a newspaper, and doing absolutely nothing. I always figured those were the cops that couldn't run or chase criminals any longer, so they were assigned to a desk. It also seemed as if they would have a chip on their shoulders and give everyone the hardest time, even when the person was the victim and not the criminal.

COFFEE

I walk up, and there are several officers at several desk. I walk over to the one officer, and he never lifts his head to address me. Well, that's like the States.

"Excuse me, sir" I say.

The officer continues to read whatever it is that he's reading. Then the desk phone rings, and he puts his index finger up as if to tell me to wait a minute. Yep, I'm wrong. They're just like the States, only sitting in different positions. I have never liked the police since the time the police were so mean to me when I was very stressed. I was getting ready for graduation, carrying all the stress of what school to go to, the entry test and paperwork, as well as supervising everyone at work. It was overwhelming. And one day at work, it appeared as if everyone called off on the same day. This forced me to work their shifts. It was stressing, and by the night's end, I apparently started saying things, threatening to kill people, and acting weird. I became aggressive and the police were called. I can't recall much of what took place, but Mom was called to the store, and she couldn't handle me; therefore, the police forced me to go to the hospital. And when I came out of it, I had been in a mental hospital for over a week. The doctors stated that I had some type of breakdown, so this has led me to not trust the police at all and some can be rude.

Now here I am, patiently waiting, and once his call is over, I expect him to help me, but instead he gets up and walks away from his desk, leaving me standing there alone.

"Uh sir, can you help me?"

The officer continues to walk away, and as he walks away, Officer Mendro comes from around the back and becks for me to follow him.

"Ms. Scott, thank you for coming, would you like a cold drink?"

I'm thinking, *Absolutely not. I'm not staying here that long. At least that's what you stated on the phone.* I shake my head no and say to him "No, thank you. What is it that you must show me, sir?"

Officer Mendro says, "Ah, right to the point."

"Yes, I'm not trying to be difficult, but I have things that I need to do."

Officer Mendro has a folder on his desk. He opens the folder and asks me if I recognize the male in the photo. At first, I was thinking, *No, I don't recognize him*, but as I looked closer, I do sort of recognize the person in the photo, but it looks as if the person is in a disguise.

I say to Officer Mendro, "I'm not sure. The person does look familiar, but they look like they are in some type of disguise. Should I know this person?"

Officer Mendro takes the photo and places it back in the folder and says, "It's not *should* you know him; the question is *do* you know him?"

COFFEE

The look on his rustic face was a bit stern, so I comment back in a brusque way and say, "Well, in that case, no. No, I don't know this individual. Are we done? Is that what you had me to come down here for?"

Officer Mendro stands up, tapping the edge of the folder on the desk and says, "Ms. Scott we were informed that you were seen walking with Ms. Fina the day we found her body. You said that you didn't know her. I'm trying to understand what's going on. Were you with her?"

"Well, I didn't recognize her from the picture. I did meet someone named Fina at the café, but that's not the name that you said at first, so I didn't put it all together. But I don't know what happened to her."

"Were you with her at all that day Ms. Scott."

I'm watching Officer Mendro, and at the same time I'm becoming uncomfortable talking to him. I go on to say, "I saw her, and we talked, and that's it."

"What was the conversation about?"

I stand up, grab my bag, and say, "Is this an interrogation or something? Because I'm feeling uncomfortable, and I need to go. I can come back and answer more questions, but I need to seek counsel first."

Officer Mendro says, "Ms. Scott, we're just asking questions. We don't want you to end up like Ms. Fina or Vaughn. That is all."

Shocked at what has just come out of Officer Mendro's mouth, I step back and say, "Vaughn? What do you mean by 'end up like Vaughn?' How is he? Has something happened to Vaughn?"

Officer Mendro looks directly at me and says, "You didn't know?"

"Know what?" I ask.

He comes back to the table, sits down, and says, "The male body that we found the other day behind the auditorium where you were seen, that had your planner in his bookbag was identified as being Vaughn."

I'm overwhelmed at what was just said. I can feel myself shaking; my palms are becoming sweaty. I ask Officer Mendro for a glass of water.

"Are you ok, Ms. Scott?" he asks.

"No, I'm not ok. You've just told me that Vaughn is dead." Looking down, while shaking my head, I say under my breath—at least I thought it was under my breath, "I just talked to him!"

"What did you say? Did you say you just talked to him…meaning Vaughn? When? Where? Spit it out, Ms. Scott. If you are withholding information from me, I promise you I'll throw your ass in jail. What is it that you know. Tell me now!"

I'm not easily scared, but I realize this is getting way out of hand; therefore, I began to tell Officer Mendro about the meeting with Vaughn and Jax.

COFFEE

When I mention that Jax was with him, he says, "That's not possible, Jax is dead."

"Yes, I thought so too, but I've seen her with my own eyes and talked to her."

"Where did you get this information from?" Officer Mendro asks.

"What info? That Jax is not dead? I told you; I've met with them."

Officer Mendro stands there looking confused while rubbing his chin. I really don't blame him because this is bad. It's all going bad, I must admit.

I'm starting to be a bit concerned, so I say to Officer Mendro, "Am I in danger? Should I be concerned?"

Officer Mendro looks back at me and says, "Honestly, I don't know, but I have a reason to believe that the person in this photo or the other one that I showed you could possibly have information that we need." He says this while showing me another photo of a person with a black hoodie on, standing outside of my apartment building. He then says, "Have you seen, or do you know this individual?"

I look at the photo and notice again that there is something peculiar and familiar about the person in this photo as well, but I can't put my finger on it; I just can't, so I shake my head once again and tell him no.

I head back over to the auditorium, and as I approach my working station, I can see that someone is in there. The closer I get, the more I can tell that the individual is rummaging through my stuff.

I yell out, "Hey!"

The individual looks up, sees me, and takes off running through the emergency exit. I run up behind him, but the person is too fast. As I look out the door while the emergency alarm is sounding, I see no one. I walk back over to my working station, and I notice that my stuff is ransacked, and a lot of my material has this oily substance on it. I pick it up and smell it. I can immediately tell that it's baby oil. Someone has ruined my material by squirting baby oil all over the place.

I'm devastated, upset, and mentally tired as well. I grab everything and just stuff all the ruined materials into the big laundry bag that I have in the corner. But as I go to grab the bag, I turn to the right, and on the floor, right by my chair, is what appears to be my black planner.

I'm thinking, *Oh my, I wrongly accused Jax of stealing my planner. What have I done? Was it here all along?*

I bend down and pick the planner up, and as I open it, scribbled on the first page are the words *I Promise*. And I notice that it's not *my* planner, it's just one that resembles it. Where did this come from?

COFFEE

I didn't have two of them. My planner was special because it was given to me by Paul years ago. I stood there thinking and recalling the last words Paul said to me were, *I Promise.*

CHAPTER TWENTY

A Message Sent

I immediately grab my phone and dial Officer Mendro. It goes directly to his voicemail. I hang up, but I am reminded of the conversation that he and I had when he first asked me to come to the station. Officer Mendro asked me if I had my planner in my possession. Now why would he ask that if he says he found a planner that appeared to belong to me?

The walk back to my apartment is brisk. My senses are heightened, and I'm taking every precaution to be aware of my surroundings. I'm looking over my shoulders, side-eyeing everyone that I pass.

COFFEE

No one is innocent; I trust no one. I *so* wished my mom was still here. This is when I could talk to her; I need her right now, I can feel the fear and trepidation overtaking me. I swallow and try to keep my head up, but the longer I think, the longer I walk. The more the tears are starting to roll down my face, the more I realize that Jax and Vaughn warned me, and now I'm in danger.

I arrive back at my apartment, go in, take a hot shower, and begin to work on the next phase of my design assignment. I'm thinking, *Just two more, and I'm out of here. I'll be on the next plane back to the States. I've had enough, and I don't want any more to do with Finland any longer. I just want to go home.*

Time is ticking away, and I now realize that I've almost finished the layout on this dark figure costume design. I still don't have a clear understanding of what Mr. Mosley is looking for, but I'm taking a shot at it. Now I need to put it all together and begin sewing it, and I'll be done. I sure hope that this is what he was referring to. If not, oh well. I'll be out of that phase and going home sooner rather than later. I came this far to win while I study abroad; I can't run home at the first sign of trouble. But I can't come here to win and end up dead either. *Home, home, I wish I were home.* As I come to an end for the night, I look down at my phone. No messages from CJ; therefore, I decide to call him myself…or maybe text him first because I don't want to come across as a booty call.

Hey there, what are you doing?

Oh, well, well, well. What did I do to deserve a text from you?

LOL, with two funny emojis is what I send back. *What are you doing this evening? Have you eaten dinner yet?*

Ms. Samantha Scott, are you asking me out on a dinner date?

Possibly.

I'm a bit famished. I could go for some good food myself, and we can talk about the next assignment.

What assignment? I ask him.

The next dress assignment that you must do.

How do you know about that? Did Tomás mention it to you?

Yeah, sure, Tomás told me all about it. So where should I meet you?

There's a nice, little café near here. I go in there every morning to—

CJ interrupts me and says, *And you take your own cup of coffee. Yeah, I know all about it.*

I'm walking to the door when CJ made this statement, but I stop in my tracks and text, *How do you know about me and the café, CJ?*

I don't know. You probably mentioned it to me, or maybe Tomás did. Who cares? I'll see you in a bit.

COFFEE

I put my phone in my pocket, and I'm in dismay because I know that I've never mentioned the café to neither Tomás nor CJ. How did he know? Has CJ been following me?

As usual, I make my special cup of coffee. I stand there and just breathe in the aroma as my mom has taught me to do. It takes me a minute or two until I hear a sound like something sliding across the floor. I peek around the corner and notice that there's another piece of paper stuffed under my apartment door.

I pick it up, and it reads. *You want answers? Go to the auditorium tonight at 10:30 p.m. Don't go in…just watch and don't be seen.*

I put the note in my pocket and walk down to the café to meet CJ. As I approach the café, I can see him through the window. How strange, CJ is sitting in the booth where I normally sit at. I walk in and walk directly over to where he is. He stands to greet me, and we sit down.

"Did you bring your coffee with you today?" He asks.

"I did, but I drank most of it while at home."

"So, what do you think?"

"What do you mean?" I ask.

"I got the booth that you always sit in. I thought you would be shocked and appreciate the effort. I guess not."

"CJ, I'm more shocked in how you knew I usually sat in this spot. Surely Tomás couldn't tell you that, and I didn't tell you. So how did you know, CJ?"

"Are you serious now? You told me on the phone when you texted me. You said you like to go to the little café and sit in the window to drink your coffee."

"I don't recall saying that. What I said was that there is a little café that I like to frequent."

"No Samantha, you clearly stated that you sit in the booth by the window. I know what you said."

"And CJ, so do I. You know what? This isn't going to work. Too much is going on, and I just can't trust anyone right now."

I grab my things to walk away, and CJ grabs me by the wrist and says, "Don't walk away from me Samantha."

Rage overcame me immediately. I looked CJ directly in the face and say, "Let my arm go. What's wrong with you?"

"What is wrong with *me*? You're the one acting all stuck up and everything. I just wanted to be your American friend. Remember? You pursued *me*!"

I snatch my arm away from CJ and say, "And it appears to be the worst decision that I've made."

I grab my things and head out the door, furious and upset, thinking, *What manner of foolishness is this? This is utterly outlandish…crazy even.*

COFFEE

Walking back to my apartment, I realize it's getting late. I decide to go over to the auditorium early to wait, just to see what the person who left the note is referring to. As I arrive at the back of the auditorium, there's no one there, which is to be expected. It's still a bit early, so I stand against the wall and just wait.

I'm scrolling through my phone, and I notice headlights coming my way. They belong to a dark colored Kia pulling up toward the back of the auditorium. I step further back so that I'm not seen; I'm stepping back but keeping my eyes on the car as it pulls up and turns its lights out.

No one gets out of the car. The windows are tinted; therefore, I can't see who's driving. I wait while the car idles. I decide to get a little closer in hopes of seeing who is driving.

Just as I get a tad bit closer, the back of the auditorium door opens, and out comes Mr. Mosley, looking very suspicious. He's bent down low as if to be inconspicuous. He's looking all around him, and suddenly he goes up to the driver's side of the car. The driver hands a brown envelope to him, Mr. Mosley opens the envelope slightly and says, "Same place, same time," and he walks back into the auditorium.

The driver backs out quickly while Mr. Mosley walks back into the auditorium, but he's so busy looking at what's in the envelope that he fails to see me walking up behind him. I'm able to grab the door just before it shuts, and I sneak in behind him.

Mr. Mosley goes straight to his office: the office where no one goes into, where the door is always closed and locked. He sits down at his desk and pours out the contents of the envelope, and I'm not surprised to see that it's full of cash. I watch him as he counts away, not aware that I'm in there with him. Once he's finished counting, he opens a wall cabinet and places the envelope in it. When the cabinet door is opened, I can see that there are several other envelopes that resemble the one in his hand.

What is Mr. Mosley doing? Is he blackmailing someone? If there was money in the one envelope, is there money in the other envelopes? Is that why he keeps his office door closed and locked? Mr. Mosley, I see you. I quickly and quietly walk backward out of the auditorium and hurry to my apartment.

Upon arriving at my apartment, I get to the door, and I could tell that my apartment door was slightly ajar. I give it a slight push, and it's dark, but I became suspicious. The hall light is illuminating enough of the apartment. I walk in, turn on the lights, and my suspicions are confirmed: someone has broken into my apartment and ransacked it.

I immediately called the police. I take a quick assessment of the room that I'm standing in. I can see that my dress—the dark figure dress—has been shredded to pieces. I slowly back out and stand in the hall, awaiting the arrival of the police.

Officer Mendro arrives and, while looking around, he says, "Samantha, Samantha, trouble follows you everywhere. So, what happened here? Do you know who would trash your apartment like this?"

"Of course not. No, I don't, and how did they even get into my apartment?"

"Well, I believe whoever it was is sending you a message, you see."

"A message?" I exclaim. "You don't think that this was just a random robbery?"

Officer Mendro looks over at me, takes his pen, and points at my dark dress design that's now shredded to pieces. He says, "I don't know any robber who would take the time to destroy a dress. We'll take uhhhh report, but I need you to come to the station, Samantha. I have more questions for you about Mr. Vaughn."

Officer Mendro's team takes several photos of the apartment, and they question me as to whether anything was missing that I could think of. While I was standing there in my own personal headspace, I look up, and who is standing at my apartment door.

Mr. CJ. Yes, CJ is standing in the doorway.

He says to me, "Sam, are you ok? What's happened in here?"

A bit perplexed to see him—and hearing him refer to me as "Sam"—I don't immediately answer him.

He takes it upon himself to walk in and again he says, "Sam, are you ok? I rushed over here as soon as I received the text."

"Text? I didn't text you." I'm sure the look on my face and my intonation relayed to him the level of irritation that I had with him for just showing up. I say, "CJ, I'm fine. For one, please don't call me Sam; and two, how did you know where I lived?"

CJ begins milling about the apartment, looking as if I have given him liberty to roam. He picks up a few of the torn pieces of fabric, sets the end table back on its legs, and gathers all the papers that were tossed around the room, placing them onto the dining table.

But CJ's next move startled me: CJ walked into my kitchen, goes directly into my left lower cabinet, and gets out a trash bag and to commence picking up the garbage. Despite the appreciation of having someone that I know here to help me, I must be true to myself. His presence makes me feel a bit protected and secure.

After he's done helping me clean up, he says to me, "Samantha, I'm sorry about earlier, I really like you, and I was feeling slightly rejected. I don't want anything to happen to you while you're here.

COFFEE

Helsinki has its share of troubles like any place over in the States; therefore, I can come off a bit strong and overprotective. Please forgive me?"

I'm a bit taken aback by his apology. I'm so focused on what has happened here that worrying about CJ and his little feelings are not a concern at this time.

Therefore, I respond with, "Don't worry about it, CJ. Yes, it's been a bit rough since I've been here; so I thank you."

CJ walks toward me, and I'm thinking, *He's going to give me a big hug or attempt to kiss me.* Instead, he walks up to me and stands directly in front of me. We're staring at each other, his strong masculine jawline eliciting a shiver of goosebumps down the sides of my arms and the middle of my spine. I immediately melt. I can feel myself displaying the shy, bashful Samantha, and I'm quickly reminded of how I'm so in love with this man, this CJ, who just earlier was a bit annoying. But I can't help it: I like him—I'm really into CJ.

CHAPTER TWENTY-ONE

Mixed Signals

The past few weeks have been interesting. Vaughn has been found dead, the crazy lady Fina is dead, my apartment has been broken into, I still haven't heard back from Jax—or anyone—that was connected to her or Vaughn, and my new boo and I have spent every waking hour together.

It's refreshing having him around. He's so handsome and so handy. Sure, we got off to a bad start, but this right here feels good; it feels right.

COFFEE

I sit on the side of the bed, preparing to get up to go cook breakfast, and I feel a finger rubbing the center of my back.

"Good morning, beautiful," he says.

I look over my shoulder with the biggest smile on my face, and I say, "Hello, handsome, I was just getting up to cook breakfast. Is there anything in particular that you'd like?"

He sits up and onto his knees behind me as his big strong hands envelop me, touching both of my arms like a warm, comforting blanket. I can feel his warm breath breathing down onto the base of my neck. He then arouses my entire insides by placing his soft lips onto my left shoulder and then onto my right. Here I am on this beautiful morning, sitting, panting in anticipation of wanting him to provide the sweetest and most passionate first fruit that he has to offer. He softly places his lips onto my right ear. And just above my lower back, I can feel the excitement that he's experiencing taking a stand.

Oh, the aroma of love is in the atmosphere: the feeling that every woman wants to experience in the waking morning is about to take place. The passion that burns within me this morning is like a forever-burning torch.

But now I can tell there is a reduction in his excitement: something's off. My fire, my torch, is doused with a tsunami of disappointment when CJ suddenly jumps down onto the side of the bed. And the first thing that comes out of his mouth isn't a soft whisper of love; it wasn't even a whisper. Instead, what comes out of his mouth causes my entire soul to halt and freeze over entirely.

He says to me hastily, "Nothing. I have errands to run. You do you. I gotta go."

What?! Is he serious?

Here I am thinking that we would have a beautiful, romantic morning, and now I'm sitting on the side of the bed, alone like a dog in heat, watching him walk away with that terribly done eagle tattoo on his left shoulder. I can tell that the tattoo was done by an amateur artist because his so-called eagle tattoo looks more like a dead vulture.

I say to myself, *Ok, Samantha stop it. You're angry and sexually irritated.* But even with the vulture-like eagle tattoo, I still like him. I really do.

CJ comes out of the bathroom already dressed, kisses me on the forehead, and walks out the door.

I remain sitting on the side of my bed, gathering my thoughts for the day. I really like my apartment here in Helsinki. It's small and quaint, but it suffices. As I sit there, I look over at my phone and notice that I've received several missed calls from Officer Mendro, and guess what? In the middle of the night I received a missed call from you-know-who: yes, the unknown number. I lift my phone to check if there are any voicemails, and sure enough, I have three. I press play, and this is what I hear:

"First call, 4:45 a.m. Samantha, this is Officer Mendro. I know it's very early, but I need you to contact me as soon as possible."

"Second call, 5:03 a.m." In his mixture of Finnish and English that I have noticed tends to surface when he's irritated, I hear, "Halloo Samantha, this is Officer Mendro again, *Mistä olet*"—he corrects himself midsentence—"where are you? I need you to soon call."

"Third call, 5:52 a.m. Samantha, you must call, you know. Call me, Officer Mendro."

I then notice that immediately after Officer Mendro's message ended, another call had come through. Did he turn right back around and call? Maybe he decided to tell me what he so desperately wanted on the voicemail since I wouldn't answer. I decided to check if the caller had left a message, and it showed another message on my voicemail. I presume that it's Officer Mendro again, but as I press play to hear the last voicemail, it's not Officer Mendro. It's a male with a mysterious voice, and he only says, "You are in danger!"

Caught off guard over what I've just heard, I pull the phone away from my ear, and I notice that the time of the call wasn't during Officer Mendro's last message. This call, the last voicemail with the mysterious voice, came through while I was listening to Officer Mendro's messages. And my phone now shows that I have two missed calls from this unknown number.

I must get dressed and get over to the auditorium to finish up with my dark figure dress that I had to start all over. After getting dressed, I grab my bags and purse, and as soon as I open my door to walk out, I'm startled when I see a tall, slender-looking male. He has his back turned to my door, and he's wearing a black hoodie pulled up over his head. I assume he's visiting my neighbor, but I notice something familiar about him and his posture.

I'm tempted to go back into the house and close my door. I don't know if this is the person that ransacked my apartment or if this someone that's coming to kill me. But instead, I walk out, and I close my door to walk pass him. I try to get a glimpse of his face, but this individual refuse to look up. I step over just close enough to bump him mistakenly on purpose, and I say, "Oh, I'm so sorry," in hopes that he would lift his head so that I could see his face. But instead, he turns further toward the wall, blocking me from seeing his face. I begin walking down the hall, but I keep looking back over my shoulder to see if I could catch him watching me or to see if he's going to knock on my neighbor's door.

But he never knocked, and I never saw his face. Careful and cautious, I continue my journey to the auditorium. Then my phone rings, I look down at it, and it's Officer Mendro.

"Hello, Officer Mendro," I say as I answer the call.

"Halloo, halloo, I've been trying to contact you. You hear my calls huh? Better yet, have you watched the news?"

"Yes, I heard your voicemails, Officer Mendro, but I've been very busy finalizing my design for the competition, and you called awfully early. What is it that you need?"

"Have you seen the news, girly? I ask of you."

"No, I haven't. Why? What's wrong?"

Officer Mendro says, "We believe that we have a serial killer in the area, and…"

Whomp, whomp, whomp, whomp, blah, blah, blah. That is what I hear because I quickly become distracted when I look across the street and see the male that was in my hall. He's walking in the same direction that I'm walking. When I left out my apartment building, he must have left as well, still with the hoodie pulled over his head. I slow down my pace in attempt to align myself to see him but to no avail.

"Samantha, are you there?"

I'm completely distracted and forgot that Officer Mendro is still on the call, and he's still talking. I heard nothing that he's said besides something about a serial killer.

Therefore, I say, "Yes, I heard you. Oh, wow." My aim is to provide him with some sort of feedback as if I were listening. I then say to him, "So now what?"

"We keep our eyes open, and everyone must be safe, Samantha. Understood?"

"Understood. Thank you for the information. I must go now." I say this and immediately end the call before the conversation picks back up.

I almost arrive to the auditorium when I look up and notice that people are running in my direction. They're crossing over onto the other side of the street, jumping on cars, running into stores, and hiding. And my being from the States and my being black has taught me one thing: you don't run toward trouble, you run from it. You don't wait to see what's going on, not when everyone is running. You can find out later what was happening.

Therefore, I take off running and attempt to cross over onto the other side of the street like everyone else, and as soon as I cross over, I see a guy with something long in his hand. It had a semicircular blade at the end of it, and he's chasing people with it. I quickly cross over, and there is a small nook between two buildings. Helsinki has a lot of those. Therefore, I dip into it to get out of the way.

The guy runs directly past me, and I'm relieved. I poke my head out to see where he's at, and he's still

COFFEE

running and swinging a long-handled sickle, usually used for cutting tall grass. From my understanding, he hasn't cut anyone, but he has truly startled everyone. I step back into my hiding spot and take a deep breath, and just when I think I can relax and start back walking to the auditorium, I hear, "Hello."

I turn around, and deep in the crevice of what I thought was just a small nook, is a tall figure standing there with a black hoodie on his head. It's the creepy guy from the hall.

Now I'm thinking, *Sam, you wanted to see who he was: now is your opportunity. But now I'm shaken and thrown off because I've run from the low-budget Edward Scissorhands, and now I'm in a dark hole with lord knows who.*

I say, "Hello," as he's coming closer into the light, still with the hoodie on and his head lowered. I can't see his face; his walk and his stature are familiar to me. And as he makes his final step to close the distance between the two of us, he lifts his hand slowly, begins to remove his hoodie from his head, and lifts his head up.

My mouth flies open, my eyebrows raise. I'm speechless for the first time in my life.

He extends his hands and embraces me, but I slowly pull away from him.

Still in shock, the words are finally able to come out of my mouth, and I say, "Paul?"

CHAPTER TWENTY-TWO

The Unwanted Guest

I'm sitting on my couch with a glass of merlot in my hand, but I'm *still* in shock. I can't believe that I saw Paul earlier, and he didn't even stay around to chat long. He just said he was in Helsinki for some time, then I watched him walk toward this dark-colored car and get in.

I asked him what does that mean, and he said he told me in the States that he was going to study abroad.

Yes, he *did* tell me, but he never said where, so I had no idea that he was here in Finland.

COFFEE

The craziest part about all of this is Paul looks different: he's not the clean-cut guy—he appeared scraggly and confused. When we spoke earlier, he just said he would explain later and come by to see me.

I believe that was him the whole time in my hall and following me, but why didn't he say anything when I walked out and bumped him? Why is he being so sneaky and mysterious? I'm scared because he threatened me before we broke up. He clearly said I would regret breaking up with him, and now he's here.

I don't need the extra stress. I must finish this dress while worrying about this serial killer. Vaughn is dead, and now Paul is in town. I've called CJ to see if he'll be coming over, but he hasn't called back. I really need to talk to him, and I want him here. Having him here makes me feel safe, and I think I need protection. Well, at least from Paul for sure. I don't know what to expect.

It's early morning, and I awake on the couch. I sit up, stretch, and realize that CJ never returned my call. I pick up my phone to see if I'd missed his call, but there isn't one missed call or text from CJ, or anyone.

I get up and go into my bedroom, and I notice that my bed appears lumpy, as if someone's tucked inside with the covers over their head. I get excited.

Surely, it's CJ. He must have come over and fell asleep, and I was knocked out from the wine and can't remember.

I don't pull the covers back because I don't want to disturb him. Instead, I decide to let him sleep while I cook breakfast. I open the refrigerator and realize that I need a few things from the market. I write CJ a quick note that says, *Honey, going to the market to get some items*. I leave it on the bedside table, and I go down to the market.

I arrive back at the apartment, and while I'm unpacking the groceries, there's a knock at my door. I go to the door, and I see another note under my door. I pick it up, and I open the door at the same time, and to my surprise it's CJ.

"What are you doing out here? Did you get up and go looking for me?"

CJ looks at me, confused, and he walks in. He's smelling so good and dressed so nice.

He turns around and says to me, "What are you talking about?"

I smile at him and say, "I ran down to the market to get some things to cook you breakfast, and I left you in the bed asleep."

"Left me in the bed to sleep? I haven't been here…who do you have in your bed!" CJ says this as he rushes to my bedroom, and I'm following behind him.

COFFEE

As we both arrive to the bedroom, the bed is made neatly, and no one is in the bed. I run over to the bed and just look. I'm shaking my head saying, "No, no, someone was in my bed this morning, and I thought it was you."

I run to the closet and open it, and then I look under the bed all the while CJ stands there watching me run around, questing after this imaginary figure that I claim was in my bed.

"So, you just have strange people in your bed?" He says.

"No, I thought it was you. I had a glass of wine and fell asleep on the couch waiting on you. When I woke up, I saw a body covered up in my bed and assumed you had slept over and left me on the couch. I was going to cook breakfast and realized that I needed to run to the market. I'd just came back when you knocked on the door. I even left you a note on the bedside table."

I go over to get the note, but there is no note there.

I look at CJ, and the look he's giving me shows that he lacks confidence in what I'm telling him. I'm sure that what I'm saying sounds insane and absurd to him, but I'm sure of what I saw.

CJ walks back into the living room and says, "I don't know what's going on, but I called you several times last night. I saw that you'd called me, so

I texted you four times. I called you, but I kept getting the voicemail, which is why I came over this morning."

I look at him confused. "You called and texted me? I don't have any missed calls or texts on my phone."

CJ reaches in his pocket and shows me his call log and the texts that he'd sent me. I look around for my phone so that I can show him that I have no calls or text from him, but I can't find it. I pick the pile of mail from the table to see if I had placed it under there; then I go back into the bedroom. I look on the bedside tables: no phone. I look under the bed: no phone.

I walk out of the bedroom, and CJ must think that I'm trying to conceal that I had someone else here. I say to him, "Apparently I've misplaced my phone. Can you call it?"

CJ dials my number, and I can hear a vibration behind me. I turn around and walk back into the bedroom with CJ following me. I listen, and the closer I get to the bed, the more I can hear where it's coming from. I pull the covers back and my cell phone is there, in the bed. It was under the neatly made covers. I lift my phone up, and the caller ID shows four texts from CJ and eight missed calls from him, including the one that just took place. I also notice a missed call from the unknown number.

COFFEE

CJ takes my phone and says, "I thought you said your phone didn't show any missed calls from me."

I couldn't do or say anything. I know he must be confused because I am too.

I tell him, "Look, CJ, when I woke up, I looked at my phone, and there were no missed calls. And when I came into the bedroom, you were—"

CJ interrupts me and says, "Don't say 'I' because I was never here." He shakes his head in disgust and says, "I thought you'd be different," as he walks out the door.

Flabbergasted at his behavior and extremely overwhelmed at this situation, I sit down on the couch, trying to collect my thoughts and recall what really took place once I came home. I had a cup of coffee, and then I had one glass of wine. I'm not a drinker, but a glass of wine wouldn't have me sounding so batshit crazy as I sound now. This is so unreal.

CHAPTER TWENTY-THREE

No Place Like Home

Evening time has come. I arrive at the café in desperate need of talking to Eevi, who is nowhere to be found. I go over to my favorite booth and plop down in frustration and confusion.

I know what I saw. I know someone was in my bed. I can't help but think that Paul is behind it, but it *can't* be Paul. How would he have gotten into my apartment...unless he's the one who broke in before. Maybe it was CJ. Maybe he really *was* there, and he behaved the way he did because I've caught him in a

COFFEE

lie. I don't know. but one thing I do know is, I can't allow this bewilderment and CJ's apparent stupefaction to distract me from finishing this dress.

I sit there drinking my coffee and thinking things through. Ideas for my dress are far from my thoughts. *Pull it together, Sam, or risk losing it all.* I continue looking out the window, and just when I look up: there she is, right there in the window looking at me with excitement that only a small child would exhibit. I stand up, to refrain from behaving in a juvenile manner, I mumble to myself, "It's Eevi. She's here! She's here!"

I beck for her to come inside the café, and she does. Eevi comes in and sits down, looking so refreshed.

I immediately blurt out, "Eevi, I *so* missed you. How have you been?"

Eevi leans over and grabs my hand and says, "I've been around here and there. How are you, my dear."

I could feel the warmth of her hands when they touched mine. My tense shoulders become relaxed. I take a deep breath and sigh, and before I can even open my mouth to say anything. Eevi is sitting on the same side of the booth with me. As the tears began to roll down my face, she takes her arms and wraps them around me tightly like a mother would do to her child to reassure her that everything would be alright now that she's here.

Eevi's concern for me is so unfeigned that I feel the only thing she can possibly do to seal the love is to kiss a boo-boo on my knee and put a bandage on it.

"It's going to be alright my dear," says Eevi. "You must press through it all. Your mom would be so proud of you."

It was like Eevi is reading my mind. The synchronicity is quite staggering to say the least, which is why I am glad she's back and isn't holding any grudges against me. I begin to tell her about everything that has transpired since the last time that we've talked, and Eevi apologized that I had to endure such things by myself. As she and I continue to talk, my telephone begins to ring.

"Hello." On the other end of the phone is the voice of Mr. Mosley. "Hello, Samantha, I want to inform you that the judging of the dark figure dress will take place in three days. I know you were a little behind, so I wanted to give you a heads-up to make sure you can have the dress finished in time. I also want to let you know that if you need to come to the auditorium to work on it this evening, you can. I'll be there, just come to the back door. You know where that is, right?"

"Mr. Mosley, yes. My dress should be finished in time. Thank you for the heads-up."

COFFEE

I end the call, and I'm a bit confused. I didn't think Mr. Mosley cared much for me, so why does he care now? Interesting.

I look over at Eevi and say, "That was Mr. Mosley, and I think he may know that I saw him the other night."

Eevi sits up in her seat and says, "Will he be a problem for you?"

"No, I don't think so. I hope not. He can cause problems for me, but I'm not going to worry about him."

"No dear, don't worry about him. What does Mr. Mosley look like?"

I thought her question of what he looks like was weird, but I told her anyway. Then I go on to tell her that I must go so that I can finish up my dress.

"Ok, well everything will work out for you, I promise."

"Oh, thank you so much, Eevi. I appreciate it."

Eevi's concern for me is so sweet; I truly appreciate having her around.

I arrive at the auditorium, and everyone's working on their designs. I go into my workspace, and as usual, I find it hard to concentrate with so much going on. Therefore, I grab my things to prepare to take them back to my apartment to work when my phone vibrates in my pocket. I look down at the number, and it's the unknown number calling me.

I answer, "Hello, who is this?"

The mysterious-voiced man is on the other end. "You know who this is. If you want answers, there is a tree near the back of the auditorium door. Beside the tree, there is a big rock. Look under the rock. Do this tonight, and you will find the answers to your questions."

"A tree near the auditorium? What is it that I'm looking for?"

As soon as I begin to ask, the caller hangs up. My thoughts are, *What is it that he thinks I need answers to? Who is this man, and how did he get my number. I wonder if I should find Eevi and take her with me?*

A few more buttons and then I can add the crinoline up under the dress to make the skirt stand out and away. I know this probably isn't what they're looking for, but this is the best that I can do for now. My design is black but it's not a "black figure dress," as Mr. Mosley has stated. I wasn't sure from the beginning as to what he meant, but I must create something to finish this round. If I can get past this round, I'll be in the finals, and I'll be so excited. The dress I was creating at first was more of what I think he wanted, but I'm going to call this dress "The Black Widow."

I finish the dress and sit back to relax for a few moments. I'm very curious of what will be under this rock. As soon as I think darkness is trying to set in,

COFFEE

I'm going down there. I really need some answers for myself and Officer Mendro.

It's late in the hour. I dozed off and really wanted to go earlier, but I'm just waking up. I put on my black joggers, black hoodie, and black tennis shoes then head down toward the front door. I look over into my kitchen and see the wood block of knives sitting on the gray-and-white checkered counter. I step back and decide to take one of the knives with me for protection, and who knows, I may have to dig something up.

I'm walking toward the auditorium; I turn the corner to go toward the back door, and I see a figure slinking away from the tree that I was told to look around. I can't quite make the person out, but from the back, the person walks like a female.

I wanted to holler out "hey," but I thought, *No, wait to see what she's doing.* The person walks away, looking back over their shoulders as if to hide from someone. I quickly cross to the other side of the street so that I can catch up to the individual; it's great that not many cars are out at this time. And in that one quick second where I look away and look back up, the person is gone, nowhere in sight.

I quickly walk over to the tree and peer around to check if anyone else was nearby. I see no one; therefore, I lift the only rock that's sitting to the left of the tree, and underneath there's a folded piece of paper. I pick the paper up and open it, and to my surprise, it's a picture: a picture of CJ and I, but in bed together.

The picture, despite how innocent it is, calls into question who is watching me and how did they get into my apartment. My heart is racing fast, and I'm looking around.

How did someone get this? Who put this here? What does this mean? But I have no answers. My thoughts are running wild. I'm thinking that I need to call CJ and tell him about this picture. Maybe the person isn't watching me; maybe they're watching CJ.

I dial CJ, and he doesn't answer, I text CJ, and he doesn't answer. His behavior reminds me of Paul so much. I don't like it when I'm being ignored, and I don't like it when someone is late to meet me or doesn't respond to my calls or texts. I text CJ to tell him that he needs to meet me at my apartment as soon as possible.

I take the picture and put it in my pocket, and as I'm getting ready to walk back, I hear cars rushing and zooming out in the distance. The sounds are getting closer and closer, and as I look up, I can see bright lights approaching me. I step back, thinking they're going to turn the corner, but instead, the two cars are coming directly at me.

The cars pull in front of me with a screeching halt, and police get out of both cars with serious urgency saying, "*Poliisi, poliisi*, put your hands up."

COFFEE

I immediately take off running. I'm so terrified that I don't stop. I know better, but I just can't get arrested over here in Finland; I have no one to help me. I ran so fast that I ended up hiding behind this building. I look back, and the police aren't on my tail, so I feel that I can take a breath.

The tears are coming down my face. I'm confused. I know Officer Mendro is behind this so I can't call him. I don't know where to turn.

I start walking back toward my apartment, and I think, *I can't go home; they'll be looking for me there.* The only thing I know to do is to call Paul.

I dial Paul's number and he immediately answers, I tell him what happened, and he tells me to come to his hotel. I arrive at Paul's hotel room, and Paul is standing in the hall waiting for me. As I walk up to him, I can feel myself becoming overwhelmed. My heart is pounding, and I can't breathe. I get up on Paul and I collapse into his arms.

While at Paul's hotel, I begin telling him about it all. I pour it out for him, so much that Paul offers me a glass of wine and tells me to relax. I know that Paul and I are not on the best of terms, but he is the only friend that I have right now. I lay out on Paul's couch, and before I know it, I fall asleep.

I don't know how long I had been asleep, but I am quickly awakened when I hear Paul say these words, "Thank you, I'll try to keep her here."

That's when I realize that Paul was on the telephone with the police. Paul isn't trying to help me; Paul was turning me in. So I jump up, grab my stuff, and run out the door.

Paul comes running behind me shouting, "Sam, Sam, come back. Where are you going?"

I take the stairs, cautiously looking to see if any officers were in the lobby area. When I don't see any, I made a quick sprint out the hotel's front door, only to run directly into two officers rushing toward me.

One says, "That's her," while the others throw me against the car and handcuff me.

I'm hysterical, anxious, and angry, but I am constantly asking, "What did I do? Why are you arresting me?" Nothing is being said, so again I say, "What did I do?"

Then it hit me: I remember being told one of the main things to learn to say in Finnish was "what did I do?" So I say to the best of my ability, "*Mitä minä tein, mitä minä tein?*"

Finally, one of the officers says, "You are hard to track down, Ms. Scott."

I wanted to say, "Go figure, dumbass, I was running," but instead I respond with, "Just tell me what I'm being arrested for."

I'm handcuffed and riding in the back of the police car when I noticed that we're following behind the police car in front of us. But when the car in

COFFEE

the front comes to the red light, it suddenly makes a right turn, and the police car that I'm riding in continues straight.

I ask the officer that's driving, "Aren't we supposed to follow behind that police car?"

He ignores me; therefore, I say again, "Sir, aren't we supposed to be following behind the other police car?"

The officer that's driving looks in his rearview mirror and tells me to hush my trap. I sit back quietly trying to figure things out, and I notice that we're slowing down and going down a dirt road.

I'm constantly asking, "Where are we going? Where are we going? I demand to know where you are taking me."

The officer driving begins to shake his head from side to side and says, "You foreigners, you Americans, always think you have the answers. You do not have the answers. Nobody wants you here. Go back home. Go back home."

I'm noticing that his accent is not as strong as the others when he talks, however, he says "go back home" with so much force that I become scared all over again. But this time, I'm not afraid because I'm going to the police station; this time, my fear was of *this* police officer. Even with fear setting in, my senses and my discernment are picking something up about him, and I don't think he's taking me directly to the station.

We finally get to the end of the dirt road and stop. I look all around, and there's nothing but trees and one big white building that looks like some old hospital or abandoned place. The area is so desolate; it's run down with no sort of life in sight.

The officer gets out, adjusts himself, and I can hear him on his phone talking. I'm very attentive to what he's saying, and it's apparent that this man is American. He has no Finnish accent as he did before.

He's speaking English very clearly, and I can hear him saying, "We're here."

I begin looking around, trying to see if there's any way I can get out of here. I look down at the police car doors, and I notice there are no handles. I'm steadily looking around. I scoot up toward the front seats, and I notice that on the dashboard is an identification card. The face matches that of the driver, but it's not a police badge. It's for an orderly or nurse of some kind.

I continue to look around and notice that there's a folder on the floor on the passenger side. There's also some type of medical bag sitting in the passenger seat of the police car, and I also notice other medical items on the floor.

My thoughts are, *Is this a police car, or is it really some type of ambulance? Is he a police officer or a medical driver?* I'm watching him as he stands outside of the car, and I'm thinking, *They never showed me any badges or even told me why I was being arrested.* Now that all the anxiety is settling, I'm taking notice that he's not wearing an official police uniform. He's no cop: he's an orderly driver, and I've been kidnapped!

A car pulls up with bright headlights, a lady gets out and walks up to the car. I can't see her face, and I can't make out her voice, but I can hear her as she says to him, "You sure this is the one?"

The driver of the car says, "Yes, we received a call from him."

"Get her out of the car," she says.

The driver comes around to the side of the car, opens the door, and pulls me out of the car. As I stand up, I stumble forward and the knife that I took from my kitchen falls out.

The lady looks down at it and tells the driver to pick it up. She then tells him to take the handcuffs off me. The driver takes the handcuffs off and pushes me toward her. I'm now standing face-to-face with this woman.

She's dressed in all white, and she's about six feet tall with long, dark hair. She has makeup on that gives her skin a pale, white, high-class gangster look along with her bright red lipstick. She has something long in her hand that resembles a long cigarette.

This is like something out of a movie, I'm thinking.

She then says, "You have really given us a runaround."

Totally confused as to what is going on, I won't give in. I refuse to die due to my weakness. I refuse to allow the foolishness of others overtake me, but what am I to do right now? I'm being arrested in a country that I don't belong in.

I say, "What is it you want with me?"

She says, "Sweetie, we're just doing our job. You must ask them on the inside."

My heart is beating at a pace consistent with someone who has just completed a full cross-country marathon. My actions, as well as inactions, are now relating nonverbally that fear has taking up residence.

Trembling and terrified, I say to her, "I didn't do anything."

The lady walks up to me, grabs my arm, and says, "Look, tell *them* that. It's out of our control... and why do you have a knife?"

Out of fear, I begin to tell her everything in hopes that she'd hear me out and understand.

I say, "I'm in school and was going to the auditorium but I was scared to be out by myself. Therefore, I took the knife for protection."

I take it that the lady has a bit of a soft spot because she then loosens her grip slightly when I mentioned school.

She asks, "What school are you talking about?"

I tell her that I am an overseas student from the United States, and I'm here to compete in the dress designer competition, and that apart from that, I know nothing. The lady looks over at the driver, and now he's hunching his shoulders and shaking his head.

The lady says, "Who were you supposed to meet? What is the person's name?"

I tell her that I don't have a name and that I received a call from a man with a weird voice.

When I mention the weird voice, the lady interrupts me. "Weird voice? What did his voice sound like?"

"It was a bit raspy like someone who had a cold."

We continue walking toward the building, and as we approach the door to enter, I begin to tell her that I'm feeling lightheaded. But in my mind, I'm still planning my escape. I allow my body to fall limp as she tells the other guy to grab me a chair.

The guy comes out with a chair, and they sit me down. I'm looking at this building, and I'm noticing that it's not the police station where I've been going to meet Officer Mendro. This doesn't look like a police station at all. The lady tells the guy to keep a watch on me while she goes in to let them know that I've arrived.

I'm sitting here, planning my next move, and I ask, "Can I get a glass of water, please?"

"Sure, I'll be right back."

All I can think about is the note that was left under my door that said I was in danger, how someone ransacked my apartment and destroyed my dress, and now look at me. All I want at this moment, is to go home. Not back to my apartment but back to the United States.

CHAPTER TWENTY-FOUR

Footprints on the Floor

I watch the man walk into the building, and at the first chance, I take off running at the fastest speed that I can. I run and run until I find the road, and I follow it, only to realize that I haven't been taken that far at all. I can see the back of the Helsinki Library, so I know where I am. I'm not far from my apartment.

I continue to run until I get back to my apartment. I'm out of breath, but I won't stop until I'm inside. When I arrive, I quickly go in, doing my best not to be seen. I don't turn any lights on. I lock the door, and my true feelings of fear and fright come streaming down my face while my body uncontrollably relaxes, my knees are buckling, and the warm feeling of urine is now running down my leg. I know that I need to get up and run to the restroom, but I can't. My body is reacting in a way that I have no control over.

I sit there gathering myself until the smell that began to waft from me is overwhelming. Not only did I wet myself, but my sphincter muscles decided that they no longer wanted to assist my rectum in keeping my bowels within my anal canal. I literally had made a mess.

I finally get up and gather myself into the shower. I stay in the shower thinking over and over, *What just happened? I'm so confused.* I stick my hand out of the shower to grab my pink bath towel that's hanging on the side of the towel bar to dry off. And as I reach for the towel, I can tell that I didn't have to reach far, the towel seemed to be right at the shower curtain, closer than what it should have been, as if someone was handing the towel to me.

I grab the towel and immediately wipe my face. My heart is racing. Someone is out there. Someone is in my apartment. I snatch the curtain back as fast as I can to see who it is, and when I open it, there's no one there.

I step out of the shower to finish drying off, and I notice that the pink towel is still hanging on the towel bar. I look at the towel that's in my hand and realize that this isn't my towel. This is the beige and burgundy towel from the towel set that I purchased for Paul's apartment back in the States. I don't recall bringing this here with me.

I bend down to dry my legs and feet off, and when I stand back up, the mirror is fogged due to the steam. I take the towel and wipe the steam away from the mirror, and when I looked in the mirror, I immediately see the reflection of the back of someone walking out of my bathroom.

I turn around and stumble back but see no one. I grab my robe and throw it on and run to the door to peek out. I see no one.

I listen suspiciously at the door before stepping out, and I hear nothing. I walk out and look around. No one is in sight. I chuckle to myself thinking, *This whole country has me going crazy. I recall Mom saying that you can be so scared that you scare yourself, and I believe this is what I am doing.*

The night is the longest night ever. I toss and turn in bed. At one point I get up and strategically place knives around the house. I push a chair up against the front and back door. I make myself a nice big cup of coffee. I then take flour and pour it on the floor all around my apartment, especially near the windows, and I walk backward to my bedroom, and get back in bed. If anyone walks around this apartment, I'll know because I'll see the footprints.

I tuck myself in my bed, cover my head, and pray that I'll fall asleep. Unfortunately, I can't sleep when I'm too hot, so that didn't work. I can't get up and turn on the fan because if I do, my footprints will mess up the untouched flour on the floor. Therefore, I lie in bed, sweat pouring off me, and I hope for the best.

I guess at some point I fall asleep because I awaken to the sound of my phone ringing. I turn over and grab the phone from my nightstand, and it's Officer Mendro. I refuse to answer because I don't know my next move. I sit there for a moment and notice that I have one message waiting. I listen, and it's Officer Mendro.

He says, "Hello, Samantha, I just wanted to check in to see how you have been and to make sure you've been safe."

I'm thinking, *Safe? So, you knew?*

His message goes on to say that he wanted to remind me that the police believe that there is a serial killer in my area and that he wanted to check on me.

He then says, "If you need me, you know where to find me."

I'm confused, you are the police, and I was just in the police custody. Surely, they've told you what's happened by now. I hang up the phone, and immediately a call comes through. It's CJ.

"Hey, CJ, how's it going?"

"Everything is ok. How are you? Are you ok?"

"Yes, I'm ok. Why do you ask?" I ask CJ this because his tone sounds so concerned.

"Well, you…um…hmm, there's a lot going on around you, so I just wanted to know."

"Oh, yeah it is, but I'm ok." CJ and I sit on the phone for a second, neither one of us saying a word. Then I say, "How are you?"

"I'm ok," he says. "I have a lot going on as well."

"Oh really? Like what, may I ask?"

CJ takes a deep breath, and he says to me, "I didn't tell you this, but my ex-girlfriend was killed, and I think the police suspect me."

I'm shocked at what I am hearing. "Wait, what? Your girlfriend? When? Who? How CJ?" The amount of intensity in my voice elevates the intonation of my speech so much that I sound like a soprano. I take a moment and repeat, "What happened?"

"No one knows as of yet; she was actually found near a dumpster by your apartment complex."

I'm thinking, *The only body that was found here was that girl, Natasha.* So I say to him, "CJ, tell me her name and exactly where she was found."

"Her name was Natasha, but we called her Fina. And she was found near a dumpster."

I'm thinking, *The person that was found near the dumpster was a white girl, and the girl he introduced me to at the school that day was a black girl named Lolita.* So I say to him, "CJ, how long had you dated her? I remember you introducing me to a black girl named Lolita."

I can tell that my line of questioning is getting under his skin. CJ says, "Lolita? Are you serious? Samantha, you have no clue. I was dating Natasha, then she goes and gets herself killed, then I met you, and now it's over with us."

I'm a bit taken aback by the brashness in his tone, but I must ask him. "Why is it over with us? I didn't know we were done."

CJ begins to scream through the phone at me saying "You had another man in your bed. You think I'm stupid. You're a whore, and I will not deal with it. You're just like those other skanks."

I pull the phone away from my ear, and CJ is so loud that I can still hear what he's saying, which is a shock to me when he says something that throws me for the loop of the morning.

CJ says to me, "So did you and your boo have a good time? I guess you got more than footprints from powder last night."

My heart skips a beat, I had totally forgotten about the flour on the floor. I lean over my bed while CJ is still ranting, and I see no footprints. I get up and walk into the living area and look around: no footprints. What is CJ referring to, and how did he know that I had flour on my floor?

I say to CJ, "How did you know I had flour on my floor?"

"What are you talking about?"

"You said I had powder on my floor...how did you know that?"

"You told me, apparently."

"I told you nothing of the sort CJ. Have you been in my apartment?"

"No, I haven't been to your apartment. You told me."

"Just like I told you about everything else that you know about me? I *know* that I haven't told you anything."

"So what are you accusing me of, Samantha?"

"I'm not accusing you of anything, but I find it interesting that you know a lot about me, and it's things that I know that I haven't told you."

While I'm making my last powerful statement to CJ, I notice that he isn't saying anything. I look at my phone, and it says, "call ended." CJ has hung up on me, the nerve of him. He can forget it now. He's fine and all, but I didn't take disrespect from Paul, and surely, I'm not going to take it from CJ.

I go to grab the vacuum out of my closet so that I can get all the flour up from the floor, and as soon as I open the closet door, *smack*...right across the

COFFEE

face. I'm hit, thinking to myself, *Man down, man down.* The hit is so hard and spot-on that I see stars. I can't see the face of who hit me, but whoever it was pushed me to the ground and ran out the front door.

I'm dazed...no blood, nothing broken. But I'm confused and one thing I can say is that I know that someone was here for sure because not only did I feel the pain, but I also see their footprints.

CHAPTER TWENTY-FIVE

Final Judging

The day has arrived, and it's final: I am officially one of the finalists for the dress designer competition. I've put everything behind me, and I've chosen to move forward. Paul is out of sight. I know he's still here, but I haven't seen either him or CJ, and CJ well, we'll just say that CJ had to go. He became a bit weird to me, and I needed to focus. I feel so relaxed, and I'm ready. I believe that I'm going to win this thing. It's been about two weeks, and I haven't gotten any crazy letters under my door. Nobody has been texting me, and even Officer Mendro has backed off. I'm focused on me, and I'm ready to win and get back to the States.

Walking into the auditorium, I see the other four finalists with their designs. As I walk past, I look at each of them, and I'm feeling confident thinking, *Samantha, you got this. None of those designs can stand up to what you've created.*

COFFEE

I go over to my station, and I'm watching as all the judges take their seats. The crowd is coming, and it's almost time to start. I set my dress up for display and take my seat to its left. In walks Mr. Mosley, and following behind him is the well-known designer, Sophie Salekari. I'm in awe. I can't believe that she's here. She's one of the younger fashion designers who has been in the spotlight since graduating in 2013. This is awesome! Knowing that she'll be looking at anything that I've created is so exciting.

Behind her is a representative of Mr. Jake Van'Iskar, who himself is not going to be judging, but apparently, he's sent someone reputable in his place. Then, right behind him, are two other individuals. I'm not familiar with those two, but it's the last person that takes me by surprise. As I look up, I take a double take because this last individual is familiar to me. It's none other than Paul.

This doesn't make sense to me. What the hell is Paul doing as a judge, and why didn't he tell me that he would be doing so? At this point I'm not even worried why he didn't tell me, but I'm very excited to see him. It's nice knowing that my ex-boyfriend is one of the final judges; that's at least one vote that I have, which will put me one vote above the others. I don't want to make a scene, but I watch him as he takes his seat. He doesn't give me any eye contact, and I get it: he doesn't want anyone to know that I'm his girlfriend. This is to prevent anyone from saying he showed favoritism.

I'm saying to myself like a high school girl, *Ok, babe, I see you. I know you did this for me. We got this, Paul, my boo.*

Mr. Mosley takes the podium and tells everyone that the judging will begin. He explains to everyone the different designs that the contestants presented. He goes on to say how long they were to create such designs. He tells them how each of us was selected and where we came from. Just when Mr. Mosely is about to introduce the judges to everyone, the door to the auditorium opens, and in walks Officer Mendro followed by two uniformed police officers. They walk over to Mr. Mosely and whisper something in his ear.

I'm wondering, as I'm sure everyone else in the auditorium is wondering, what's going on. As Officer Mendro continues talking to Mr. Mosely, he takes a piece of paper out of his pinstriped jacket pocket and hands it to Mr. Mosely. Mr. Mosely steps down and walks over toward Paul.

I'm thinking, *What is going on?*

But Mr. Mosley walks directly past Paul while the police officers and Officer Mendro follow behind him. No one says anything to the contestants, and no one addressed the crowd. Mr. Mosley takes them into the back where his office is located, and he grabs his briefcase from his desk. Mr. Mosley comes back in and tells everyone that the judging must be postponed. He walks out with Officer Mendro, and the other officers follow closely behind them.

The rest of us are confused. Is Mr. Mosley being arrested? What's going on. The designers are looking around, and just when we think that there will be no judging, in walks the director of the school. I don't recall her name, but she looks very Eastern European compared to some of the other women that I've encountered here. She's even blonder and slimmer, maybe a model even.

She stands before everyone and tells them that despite what Mr. Mosley has said, the judging will continue as planned. She never tells us what is going on with Mr. Mosley, and the judging continues.

I'm happy that my design was chosen, but it has tied with another designer, a young lady who I haven't seen much of. I think she may be American, but who knows? I never had time to get to know anyone. Nonetheless, I'm excited. I'm overjoyed, and I must admit, I'm confident that I'll win.

The crazy part is that some smart individual has decided to let the crowd judge at the annual Helsinki Runway Walk. This is the annual show where all the top designers come out and showcase their new line of clothing. This is awesome! It's more publicity and the opportunity to get discovered by some top designers. We had to leave our designs at the auditorium because they didn't want us adding or taking away from what has already been judged. I feel comfortable with that, knowing that my apartment has been compromised with my previous design destroyed before. The Runway walk is this weekend, and I have time to relax and prepare myself for the big day.

As everyone begins to disperse from the auditorium, I try to catch up with Paul, but he leaves immediately after the judging. I wanted to thank him for the vote, so I text him and ask if we can meet up that evening for dinner.

Paul doesn't text me back, but CJ does. He's asking if I could meet him later for coffee. I don't respond right away because I'm waiting on Paul to respond to my text.

I arrive at my apartment, and as I'm getting ready to change clothes, I reach into my pocket, and there is the picture that was left for me by the tree a while back. I'd completely forgotten about this picture. I look at it, and I'm still wondering who could have taken this picture of CJ and me in bed together. I decide to text CJ, and I agree to meet with him.

Yes, we can meet, but let's do dinner. I just had a cup of coffee already.

CJ texts back, agreeing, and says eight tonight. I go into my bathroom to take a shower. As I walk into

COFFEE

the bathroom and turn the light on, I'm startled by what appear to be pictures that are taped all around my bathroom. I walk up and take one down so that I can see what they are pictures of. And to my surprise, they're pictures of CJ and me like the one of us lying in bed. They're photos of us meeting at the café, walking down the street...so many pictures of just the two of us, and they are taped around my bathroom.

I'm furious and terrified at the same time. Who took these pictures, and how did they get into my apartment? I begin to take the pictures down, and the tears are falling. I feel like I'm being harassed and possibly stalked. On top of it all, I have no idea of who it could be. How can this individual continue to gain access to my apartment without me knowing. I call CJ.

"CJ, I need you to come to my apartment immediately."

CJ, sounding so unbothered, says, "Why? What's going on? I thought we were meeting for dinner tonight."

"CJ, there's something going on that I need you to see."

He sighs as if I'm becoming a bother to him, but he responds with, "Ok, I'm on my way."

CJ arrives at my apartment. He's wearing a red sweater that's fitting his body like a glove. I recall the first time that I saw him, he had on another sweater that fit him the same way. Oh, he's so handsome and muscular.

I let him in and show him the pictures, and he's just as confused as I am. He begins walking around the apartment. He's looking under the bed, looking in the cabinets, and then he says, "Let me see the pictures again."

I show him the pictures and he inform me that all the photos are taken from a certain angle. CJ walks into the bedroom, looks up at the ceiling then back down at the bed.

He does this again and says to me, "Get me a chair to stand on."

I ask him what for and what he was doing.

He turns to me and says, "Do you want help or not? Just get the darn chair, would you?"

I go into my dining area, grab a chair, and hand it to him. CJ stands up in the chair and begins to twist the smoke detector so that it opens.

As soon as CJ gets it open, he says, "Oh, my!"

I look up, and I can see a small, tiny camera affixed in the smoke detector.

CJ says, "Look, it's a camera."

Agitated, I quickly snap at him, and I say, "I see that it's a camera CJ, but how the hell did it get there? And who put it there?"

CJ looks over at me and says, "Why are you mad at me? How am I supposed to know? This is your apartment. I'm in these photos as well, and I don't like it. Are you doing some crazy stuff in this apartment that I don't know of?"

I find no humor in CJ's comment, and I just say to him, "How could I have taken the photos of us in the café and walking the street, CJ? Think, man, think. Just take it down immediately, CJ."

I decided to go ahead and call Officer Mendro. His call from the other day was a bit off, but maybe he's trying to help me. And right now, I'll take it. I call Officer Mendro while CJ takes down the camera.

CHAPTER TWENTY-SIX

The Photoshoot

After speaking with Officer Mendro, I inform CJ that he's on the way. CJ seems a bit nervous, and he tells me that he won't be here when the officer arrives.

I ask, "Why not? You're a witness of where it was located, and you're the one who removed it. You need to be here."

"I don't like police, and I'll leave a statement. But I can't be here when they arrive, and that's it."

"CJ, I need you to—"

COFFEE

CJ interrupts me and says, "You *need* me? You need me to what? Nothing. I know nothing, and I don't want to be a part of this—"

"This *what* CJ? You *are* a part of it. You're in the pictures, just like I am, and you found the camera."

CJ walks up in my face as if I didn't understand him before. He becomes very aggressive and loudly says, "I will not be a part of this, and if my name is mentioned, I will say that you're a liar and that you paid me to take these pictures with you."

I'm so nervous and appalled at his behavior. He immediately storms out. I don't even get a chance to ask him why he would say something like that. And why is he so against being here when Officer Mendro arrives. Something isn't right with CJ, and currently I don't have the time to worry about his mess.

Just when I'm about to sit down, there's a knock at my door. I get up and walk over to open the door, and right there in my face is another note that's been slid under my door. I pick the note up and open the door to see Officer Mendro and his cronies standing there.

"Hi, Ms. Scott, can we come in?"

While crumbling the note into my pocket I say, "Yes, come in, Officer Mendro. Have a seat."

I'm expecting that Officer Mendro will either arrest me immediately or ask about the arrest the other day, but instead he says, "So, what is it that has you so spooked?"

I hand Officer Mendro the pictures and begin to explain to him where they were found.

"Who is the guy in the picture with you?" He asks.

"Oh, that's CJ; he's sort of like a boyfriend of mine."

"So, are you all not together any longer?"

I rub my hand through my hair and explain that we aren't really an item, that we just keep each other company when we need to. Officer Mendro hands the pictures to one of his officers that's still standing, but I have my eyes on him because he's walking around and searching my apartment in his own stealthy way.

I say to Officer Mendro, "He's the one that found the pictures, but he couldn't be here today."

"And why is that?" He asks.

"Well, he had another appointment and couldn't miss it."

Officer Mendro looks over at the officer that's sitting down beside him.

I ask, "Officer Mendro, is there a problem with him not being here?"

"I guess not. Can you provide me with CJ's full name?"

I look at Officer Mendro and then the other officer that has walked into my bedroom. He's not touching anything but he's looking up at the ceiling just like CJ did, and he's taking notes. It never dawned on me that I really don't know CJ's real name. I just know him as CJ from the States. I'm so embarrassed, but then I'm thinking, even if I knew it, I wouldn't give it to him because CJ was adamant that he didn't want to be involved.

Therefore, I say to Officer Mendro, "CJ isn't important. I just wanted you to be aware of what's taken place."

Officer Mendro nods his head and stands up. He walks into my bedroom as if he's taking a sneak peek. He too, looks up to the ceiling and says, "So the camera was found in the smoke detector you say?"

"Yes, that's where it was found."

"And CJ, your bed partner…I'm sorry, your boyfriend-like guy, found it, correct?"

Again, I say, "Yes. That's correct."

"And this CJ, he had an appointment and couldn't be here today, correct?"

I'm looking at Officer Mendro, and I say, "Yes, Officer Mendro, all of that is correct. We went over that already."

Officer Mendro now holds the pictures in his hand, and he says, "Have you noticed that none of these pictures give a clear image of CJ's face except one? It's either sideways or the back of his head."

I take the pictures back from Officer Mendro, and I look at them and say, "Is there a point you're making?"

Officer Mendro walks over to me, takes one picture out of my hand, and says, "Does it seem like—the only picture that shows his face, even though its blurred—your friend CJ is looking in the direction of where the smoke detector is at? It's almost as if he knows that there's a camera there."

I take the picture back, and I look at it, but while I'm doing so, Officer Mendro lies in my bed. He's trying to get the camera angle of the way we were lying.

He asks, "Do you sleep on the left side or the right side of the bed?"

"I sleep on the left side; again, what is your point?"

"It's interesting that the way your bed is positioned, the camera gets a good angle of anyone in the bed, but for it to only get half of the person on the right side, that would mean that that individual intentionally made sure they were out of the camera's line of sight. Where's the camera that you discovered?"

I walk over to the table and look around: no camera. I look on my nightstand: no camera. I'm searching all around the house and can't find the camera. Then I realize, CJ must have taken the camera with him. I surely don't want to tell Officer Mendro that CJ has the camera; he's already showing conjecture when it comes to CJ, and I don't want to add to it. But what else can I do.

COFFEE

I look at Officer Mendro and flat out lie. I say to him, "Camera, what camera?"

Officer Mendro looks over at his partner and says, "The camera that you claimed your boytoy discovered."

"Oh, *nooo*, I said CJ didn't *discover* a camera; he looked all around, even in the smoke detector, and didn't find a camera is what I meant. Maybe I confused you when I called because I was still upset."

Officer Mendro's face expresses doubt, but he says while nodding his head, "Maybe, yeah, maybe. If we don't find a camera in here, that means that whoever took the pictures must have been in the house every time the pictures were being taken. I would suggest contacting the *voukraisäntä* to change the locks."

The expression on my face clearly shows that I have no idea of what a *voukraisanta* is. That's when one of the officers that were with him says, "Landlord," and walks away.

Officer Mendro says all of this, and he then walks toward the door. He says, "You know, I'm not buying anything that you're saying. Oh, and your boyfriend, CJ, is already under investigation." He never turns around to look at me, he just says this and walks out.

I stand there looking dumbfounded because of what he has said, but also because Officer Mendro never said anything about me getting away from the officers. This has me really confused. Were they really police?

I close the door, thinking, *How can you have sex with someone and have no knowledge of his real name?* And on top of that, it appears that I may need to be a bit concerned about what CJ knows and what he's doing.

I know I need to talk with CJ about everything, but I just need a break. I go into the kitchen and make myself a huge cup of Mom's coffee, and I sit down on the couch to relax my mind and enjoy the idea that my dress design has been chosen. I never got a chance to just celebrate, but who would I celebrate with? CJ? Paul? I tried, but this whole stalking issue has been too much.

I sit and I let out a huge laugh, I can feel how big my smile is, but I also can feel the tears welling up in me. Suddenly the laughter stops, the smile dissipates, and the tears take center stage in my life. Oh, this visit has been so bitter-sweet. I truly enjoyed coming here to compete, but I so miss my mom. She would've been so proud of me. When I return to the States, I'll stop by the school. Mrs. Voltsclaw is going to be so proud, and the school will be proud that I represented them very well. I'm sipping on my coffee, allowing the aroma to excite my nostrils. I hold my head back just like Mom, and I take deep breaths.

CHAPTER TWENTY-SEVEN

What is your name?

I've done my one errand, and I must get all my paperwork signed from the professors at the school just in case I don't win this competition. If I lose, I'm allowed to finish the semester and then fly back to the States...or I could leave immediately, if I choose. But because I'm part of the school's special designer program, my rent is covered by the school. So if I lose, they will only allow me to stay in the apartment rent-free for one month. Afterward I'll be responsible for paying my own way. From my understanding, those that lose usually fly back to their country immediately to avoid the bills, and I think I'll take that route if I lose. But I don't plan to lose.

I'm walking back to my apartment when I look over into the café window and see someone that resembles Jax. I go into the café, and sure enough, it's Jax. I rush over to her and immediately want to hug her, but Jax isn't looking too friendly.

I sit down where she is, and I say, "Where have you been? Have you heard Vaughn is dead? People think you're dead, and so much is going on. You must talk to this officer."

I look into my purse to hand her Officer Mendro's card, but Jax puts her hand up and stops me.

She looks around to ensure no one hears us, and in a whisper, she very firmly says, "I won't talk to him, and neither should you."

"Officer Mendro is a police officer. Jax, he's been assigned to the case, and he's helping. I know he's a bit weird, but he's the police. You must let him know that you're alive."

Jax pulls her hoodie up onto her head. Her eyes appear a bit fixated on something behind me. I turn around, but I see nothing that stands out.

I ask her, "Are you ok?"

No response.

I ask her again, "Jax, are you ok?"

She continued to stare, grabs her things, and just walks away without saying goodbye or anything.

Strange and peculiar, that Jax is. I watch her walk toward the door, but I'm not sure if I turn my head and lost sight of her because I never see her walk out the door nor walk onto the street.

Unsure as to where she went, I gather my belongings and walk toward the door. The barista Olson is standing with both hands on the counter, and he's looking straight ahead.

I lift my hand to give a wave goodbye, and I say to him, "Have a good day."

He never responds or even acknowledges me. I'm *so* ready to go back to the States. I can't say I've enjoyed my stay here in Helsinki. It's been trouble since I've gotten here. I just want to be home around some friendlier faces and the people that I know.

I text CJ and get no response. I call Paul: no answer. No one is around. I decide to call Officer Mendro and inform him about the paper that was under my door with the name on it. Officer Mendro doesn't answer so I leave him a message.

"Officer Mendro, this is Samantha. I don't know if this is of any importance or not, but I meant to tell you when you had stopped by my apartment that I received a note stuffed under my door. When I opened the note, it had the name Joseph C. Mosley Jr. on it. I don't know who that is. Maybe it means something to you. Please give me a call when you are available."

COFFEE

As soon as I finish leaving the message, my phone rings, and it's Paul.

I answer, "Hello, Paul."

Paul sounds very distant on the other end, but he says, "Sam, why did you leave the other day? You called me to help you, then you ran off. Whatever is going on with you, just be careful. Someone is attempting to sabotage you and your chances of winning the competition. I don't know who, but I overheard someone stating that there has never been a winner from the States, and there will never be one. Therefore, I want you to know that despite our issues, you have my vote."

I'm listening to what Paul has said and how he'll vote for me. His statements leave me misty eyed, but I'm a bit distracted because Paul's conversation seems a bit off.

I thank Paul, and I say, "Paul, I appreciate your help, but they will have a winner from the United States this year for sure."

Paul gives a deep sigh and says, "Sam, just be careful."

"I will, Paul. I will."

One thing for certain is that Paul knows that I don't scare easily. So for him to call and make that statement, he probably knew that it wouldn't do anything but cause me to work even harder. However, even with that, the dress is done, and it's in the hands of the school and judges. There's nothing more I can do to seal the win. Paul's vote will help, but there are other judges that my dress needs to impress.

I'm finishing the call with Paul, and he and I are agreeing to meet tonight for dinner when my other line rings. I look down at my caller ID, and it's Officer Mendro. I answer immediately.

"Officer Mendro, thank you for returning my call."

"Not a problem, Samantha. I've listened to your message, and you stated that the name on the paper was John C. Mosley Jr. I don't understand what you mean when you say you do not know who this person is."

"Well, I don't. The only person I know with the last name Mosley is the teacher at the school."

"Samantha, you really should vet those you sleep with a little more."

"Officer Mendro, if you have something to say, just say it."

"Aren't you dating CJ?"

"Yes and no. I've told you that we're friends but not dating. Besides, what difference does it make?"

"Well, it makes a helluva a lot of difference when you know the name of the people that you are sleeping with."

"Again, what are you saying? Spit it out."

"I'm saying that when I went up to the school to inquire about CJ, I found out a lot of pertinent information."

"Information like what."

"For one, he has a sister. And for two, his parents—or should I say, his parent—works at the school."

"Wait, are you telling me that CJ has a sister and he never told me? Who is she, and who is his parents?"

"I haven't met her, all I know is that she's competing in that dress competition with you," says Officer Mendro. "I figured you already knew all about this."

"No, I had no idea about his sister or parent. Which parent? Well, I guess it doesn't matter."

"Ms. Scott—"

I interrupt Officer Mendro and say, "There you go with that 'Ms. Scott' mess. It's Samantha. Samantha, please."

Officer Mendro chuckles and says, "Samantha, you really need to do your homework on the men that you interact with, especially being from another country. CJ, your friend is the son of Mr. Joseph C. Mosley Sr., one of your instructors."

Shocked at what I'm hearing, my mouth hangs open. I say, "Wait, are you serious? CJ is Mr. Mosley's son? Nooo, no way. Can't be. He never said anything, and he surely doesn't look anything like him. I've never even seen them interact."

"Well, it's true. That's his son."

"Well, I must go handle some business. I wish you well in the competition tomorrow, but more so, I want you to be careful, Ms. Scott…I mean, Samantha. There are a lot of unanswered questions, and with the latest info and the arrest of Mr. Mosley, I don't know what to think."

"I hear you, sir," I say to him, but my thoughts are all over the place.

CJ is Mr. Mosley's son? I still don't believe it. Does Tomás know this? He hasn't said anything to me about it. Also, CJ never told me that he has a sister, and he surely never said that the sister is competing against me. This makes me uncomfortable, and now I'm wondering if CJ broke into my apartment and destroyed my dress to help his sister win the competition. Was that the plan all along? To woo me and sidetrack me so that his sister could win? Like Officer Mendro said, there are a lot of unanswered questions here.

CHAPTER TWENTY-EIGHT

Helsinki Runway Walk

It's here. The day has arrived, and I'm feeling pretty good. My clothes are packed, even though I'm positive that I'll walk away with the win. I take my shower, and I'm preparing to get dressed. I have this beautiful, archaic pattern midi dress that I created for myself to wear. I have my hair pinned up with a silver butterfly clamp on the left side of my head to give me a slightly sophisticated appearance. I normally don't wear makeup, but I'm wearing it today. I hear that the television crews and newspapers are always in attendance for this event. Besides, this is one of Helsinki's biggest events that many look forward to; it's great that they're including the dress competition. Oh, how I wish my mom were here to enjoy in the festivities and to celebrate with me.

I'm standing in the mirror, looking at myself. I'm pretending to do the celebrity wave, going over the speech I would say once I win. I know there won't be a speech, but it's how I've envisioned everything. I'm waving my hand with all fingers tightly touching one another. I'm practicing my unpretentious royal smile that will grace my face as my name is called. This is going to be a great day; I'm so looking forward to it being over.

I check the clock: it displays 9:44 a.m. I know I'm up early, but I couldn't sleep. As a finalist, I'm expected to be at the location by eleven so that they can go over what to expect. The judging will start promptly at noon. From what we were told, once I arrive, I'll be given access to my dress so that I can go over it one last time.

Even though I have some sweet sounds of jazz blasting from my radio, my stomach is in knots and feels like it wants to push out anything that's swimming around in it. I lean over the porcelain toilet to give it a try, but nothing comes up. I'm dry heaving but still nothing. But as my stomach takes a shot at the final dry-heave, I'm startled by the sounds of the symphony church bells. I'm confused because they normally only play at noon. Why are they ringing at 10:00 a.m. Maybe it's because of the big Runway festival, who knows? I continue to put the finishing touches to the beauty of who I am, and I look over at the television, which is muted.

The news anchor is broadcasting live from the Helsinki Runway festival, and I notice that he's interviewing a young lady who is standing beside a dress. I immediately turn my radio all the way down and turn my television all the way up, and that's when it happens. That's when I become aware. I'm hit in the gut when I notice that going across the ticker at the bottom of the television were the words, *Winner of the Helsinki Runway Competition, Ms. Lolita Mosley, from Princeton University.*

I look at the picture closely, and it's the girl that I saw with CJ when I first met him. The feeling of life leaving my body comes across me quickly. I grab my purse and rush down to the festival, and as I'm walking up, I see CJ, Mr. Mosley, Tomás, and Paul.

Paul comes over to me shaking his head in disgust. The first thing that comes out of his mouth is, "I can't believe you didn't show up for the competition. I thought you really wanted this."

I'm still in shock, because I'm now realizing what has taken place.

COFFEE

I say to Paul, "I thought the competition was at noon and that I had to be here at eleven. No one told me of the time change."

Paul looks at me, confused, and says, "Sam, it's 1:15. You've missed the competition. They deemed you a no show. I called you several times, and you never answered. I texted you, and there was no response. And as the rules state, the designer must present their own dress. Where were you? Why didn't you show?"

I look down at my phone, and I see no calls or texts from Paul. I'm not concerned about the calls, but I immediately walk away from Paul and over to Mr. Mosley who had his arm around Lolita and who is standing beside CJ. All three had such smug looks on their faces as I approach them. Mr. Mosley is the first to say anything.

"Samantha, it's such a shame that you were unable to finish the competition. I was sure that you would be the one who would break the cycle."

"Cycle? What do you mean by 'cycle'?"

"Well, for years Helsinki Runway has been won by someone from Finland. We've never had an American to win, but my daughter, Lolita"—he chuckles— "really surprised me, and she won it all."

"Lolita, how could she have won? That's impossible. No, this was a setup. I was supposed to have been here. My clock, my clock."

As I'm attempting to state my case to Mr. Mosely, one of the judges comes over with the final design that won the competition, and he says, "Ms. Lolita, this design was everything. The way you executed your ideas were just superb. I don't think there was any other design that came close to yours. You should be extremely proud."

Lolita looks over at me with a smile and says to the judge, "Thank you, sir. I couldn't have done it without my dad and brother. It was all part of our plan for me to win by any means necessary, so I worked very hard to win."

To my surprise, the dress that Lolita submitted is identical to the dress that was destroyed when someone broke into my home. I become furious; therefore, I yelled out at Lolita.

I say, "That is *my* dress. You stole my dress."

Lolita takes a step back and says, "Whatever do you mean? I stole nothing."

I walk up closer to her and say, "Admit it, you are a cheat. You all planned this."

Lolita never acknowledges me, turns, and walks away. Then, as the judge goes to hand her the dress, I snatch it out of his hands and say to him, "This is not her dress. This belongs to me. It's mine, all mine, I tell you."

The judge and everyone else become quiet and all eyes are now looking at me.

"What are you all looking at? This is my dress. I created this, not Lolita. This was for me to submit." I'm saying this while I'm crying and extremely emotional.

Mr. Mosley begins to walk past me, and he says, "Well, dear, you didn't show up on time, so what were we to do? But it's clear that this wasn't of importance to you." He says this as he embraces Lolita and giving a sheepish and suspicious look.

I look over at Paul for help, but Paul is standing there with such a disappointed look on his face.

"Paul…Paul, I didn't."

But before I can finish my statement, Paul throws his hand up toward my face. While shaking his head, he shows me how disgusted he is of my behavior. He turns and walks away from me as well.

With tears in my eyes, I slowly begin to walk away until I notice a crowd of people standing off to the side. I begin to wonder what's taking place, and when I look closely, I notice that one of the individuals resembles Vaughn. Surely this isn't Vaughn…he's dead.

But as the individuals moved around more with their laughter and banter, I notice that Jax and CJ are in that crowd as well. *Wait, this can't be*, I begin to say to myself. Vaughn is dead. How can this be? The laughter and high fives that CJ is giving Paul is unnerving, but what sends chills down my spine—and possibly sends me over the edge—is when Lolita walks up and kisses Paul dead on the lips.

It's then that I begin to wonder if I was setup. Was this to get me out of the competition? The amount of anger that builds up in me is unreal. I feel horns popping out of my head and steam coming from my nose. I'm now enraged because they all were in on this, and I must confront them. I must.

Therefore, I storm over to where they're standing, and as soon as I approach them, CJ turns around and blocks me from getting any closer.

I begin to push him in the chest and say, "Were you a part of this mess? Tell me, were you a part CJ? Was our relationship just so your sister could win?"

CJ grabs my arms and says, "Samantha, calm down. What's wrong with you?" CJ says this as if he has no idea of why I'm so angry.

"You know what's wrong with me. You and your family set me up, and you pretended to like me to get me distracted so that your sister could win the competition."

"My family? What are you talking about? I really don't know you."

I stare CJ in the face and know that I'm being bamboozled. Before I knew it, I jump at CJ and begin choking him. Security and others nearby grab me and try to hold me down, but I'm able to get away. I run so fast down the corridor and back to my apartment.

My heart is heavy, and I'm appalled at the nerve of everyone. Everyone pretended to be friends with me only so Lolita could win. It was all a plan to keep me confused and distracted. Vaughn is alive. Jax is alive. And I bet Fina is as well. I can't believe that all of them were in on this scam just to beat me in a competition.

I arrive at my apartment and there is a note at the door, when I open it, it reads, "*I Promise.*" I collapse onto the floor of my apartment, and I cry and cry until the banging on my door stops the tears from flowing. I can hear people at the door saying, "Open up, it's the police."

What would the police want with me? I didn't hurt CJ; I barely choked him. I didn't steal a design…Lolita stole mine, but I'm from the United States. I'm not opening this door.

"Samantha, open this door, or we will kick it in. This is Officer Mendro."

The banging on the door becomes more and more intense. I'm in a full-throttle panic. I can't breathe or think. I can't go to jail over here in Finland, so I grab a few of my items and grab a knife. I'm feeling dizzy and dry mouthed. I can't focus. I'm hyperventilating. I must get out of here.

So I ran to the back door, and as soon as I open the door, I see a figure dressed in all white. And the next thing I know, it feels like something sticks me, and all I can see is the inside of my eyelids.

Solipsism
November 27, 2016

Breakfast is ready. Breakfast is ready.

I'm hearing this over in my head. I turn over, and the clock shows 8:17 a.m. I need to get up.

I hear again, "Breakfast is ready, Sam. Get up."

It's Mom. She's gotten up early, and she's cooking breakfast. I need to hurry up and get dressed. I love eating Mom's breakfast foods; she always makes something totally different from the norm. I get up and go downstairs for breakfast, and Mom is cooking away, as usual, in the kitchen.

"Good morning, Mom. It smells so good in here. What're you cooking?"

Mom continues to cook and says, "Nothing fancy, just eggs, bacon, sausage, fried potatoes, fried green tomatoes, and Belgian waffles. Would that be enough for you?"

"Would it be enough?" I say. "Absolutely. But what has you so excited and up and cooking at this time of morning?"

"Well, I want us to celebrate my baby getting accepted to study abroad at that fancy, dandy designer school, Samantha. Momma is so proud of you, babe. You're really making a name for yourself."

COFFEE

I smile at Mom. I walk over to hug her as she's still standing at the stove cooking. I wrap my arms around her from the back, and I close my eyes. She smells so good. Her skin is so soft to touch, and I'm just holding her. The warmth, the love: I can feel it. I can hear her breathing, but her breathing sounds a bit odd. It sounds heavy at first, then it's starting to sound rumbly, almost like a humming sound.

I ask, "Mom, are you ok?"

Mom never answers. The smell of the breakfast is no longer a bouquet unto my nostrils. In fact, I don't smell anything at all. The warmth from her body is no longer there. The softness no longer exists. What's going on?

I then open my eyes, and I notice that I'm standing in front of the refrigerator. My arms are wrapped around myself. I call out to Mom, but she's nowhere in the house. I lean against the kitchen wall. I'm exhausted. The wall appears to no longer want to hold me. My body begins to slide down, and I'm now on the kitchen floor, and I'm crying my eyes out.

I look around, and I'm still in Helsinki, in my apartment. No Mom, no breakfast, no Paul, not even a call from CJ. Just me, surrounded by nothing and no one. I'm alone.

CHAPTER TWENTY-NINE

Homestead MI
April 7, 2017

"Nurse, nurse, can you please come here?"

"Hello, Ms. Scott, how may I help you?"

"I want to know when the doctor will be around. I need to get out of here. I have things to do now that I'm back in the States."

"Ma'am, I don't know when you will be leaving. You must discuss that with the Doctor."

"When will he be making his rounds?" I ask.

COFFEE

"I don't know, but he'll be in to see you soon."

I'm looking at the male nurse, and I notice that the name on his ID says *Tomás*.

I smile slightly, and through a soft mumble I say, "Tomás, you are my nurse?"

The nurse standing at my bed looks up from the medical board that he's reading and gives me a faint smile. I'm thinking, *Well, he's not too talkative*. Therefore, I say to him, "Tomás, why are you looking at my chart? You aren't allowed to do that. And how did you know that I was here?"

The nurse continues to write on the board, then a short time after he looks down at me and says, "How are you this morning?"

Ok, I'm thinking, *So you don't want to answer my questions*. Therefore, I say, "Tomás, I don't know what kind of game you're playing, but I'm tired and I won't participate in it. Did Paul put you up to this?"

"You're going to be fine ma'am. Do you need anything?"

I'm surprised to hear him saying anything. Let me see if he can find out when I'll be leaving. As Nurse Tomás continues to update my records, I hear a voice that sounds familiar and seems to be coming closer. Just when Nurse Tomás steps away from the bed and pulls the curtain so that I can't see anyone, I can hear him say, "Dr. Mosley, how are you doing today?"

I'm thinking, *Dr. Mosley? Ok, so this is crazy. This voice sounds like Mr. Mosley from over at the school. Surely this can't be him, and if it is, why is he here? He knows he's not welcomed, and he's no doctor. First Tomás as a nurse, and now Mr. Mosley is my doctor? What's really going on?*

I can't see the Dr's face just yet, but I can hear the conversation that he's having with Nurse Tomás.

He replies to nurse Tomás, "I'm doing well, how is the patient coming along?"

"She's fair...still confused," says the nurse.

I notice that he has started to talk to Dr Mosley in a very soft tone, almost as if they're whispering. I can't make out what they're saying, but I did hear the nurse say to the doctor that "she's beginning to ask questions, as is to be expected."

"Yes, I expected that much," is what the doctor says. "Well, let's see what we got here."

He and Tomás come from behind the curtain, and I look up and see a man who's about 6'2 with a muscular build and long hair pulled back into a ponytail.

I'm thinking, *Wait a minute here. He's handsome, he's built, he has long hair, and his name is Mosley... but this is very off-putting. I don't like this at all. Who's behind this fiasco? Is this part of the competition?*

All these questions are going through my head. First Tomás appears as my nurse, and now the doctor

COFFEE

looks like my CJ. This is a bit eerie. Am I dead? Am I dreaming? What's really happening?

Ok, I get it: this is some kind of joke. Paul put them up to this. I know it, Paul is a joker. But honestly, I can't believe how great the resemblance of them both are. Should I just play along or demand that I'm too tired for this? Then wait, can this all be in my head? Did I fall and hit my head? I must admit, I've spent a decent amount of time here in Finland under some stressful situations, and my mind could be playing tricks on me.

Dr. Mosley walks over to the end of my bed and says, "Ms. Scott, how are you feeling today?"

"I'm doing great doctor," I say as I continue to play their game. "When can I get out of here? I need to get back home; I'm still tired and jetlagged from my flight from Helsinki."

Dr. Mosley is looking at me nodding his head. Nodding his head is fine, but I need answers. I need him to tell me when I'll be going home.

"Ms. Scott, we don't know when we can release you."

"What do you mean? Why am I here?"

"You don't recall, Ms. Scott?"

"Apparently not. I asked why I'm here, so are you going to tell me…Mr. Mosley?" I say this with a hint of sarcasm, because by now I'm playing their game.

"Well, you were brought here because you were a bit out of it, and we want to make sure that you are ok. Therefore, we admitted you and are still observing you."

"No, Dr. Mosley, I need to go home." I begin to say this over and over, and the tone of my voice elevates each time it's said. "I need to go home. I need to go home, and I want to go now!" That's the last time I say this because I'm sure that I'm yelling like some sort of mad woman.

I can't believe my behavior. It's not like me to become this way with others, but I've been fooled. After my display of aggression, I can't believe what comes out of my mouth next.

"I tell you what. Either you tell me when I'll be getting out of this hell hole, or I'm going to walk clear out of here. Do you understand me, CJ? I know it's you."

I say this and attempt to sit up enough in the bed so that I can look this Dr. Mosley square in the eyes. This energy that I display is the most I can muster up to attempt to irritate them. I know I'm doing this to get their attention, but they're acting as if they're not hearing me. Therefore, I continue to scream, but my screaming doesn't seem to bother them. Instead, Dr. Mosley looks away from me toward Tomás and nods.

Tomás then takes a syringe out of his pocket and injects me in my arm. I attempt to reach over to stop

COFFEE

him, but my arm feels heavy. I look over at my arm and notice that I couldn't move my arm because it's strapped to the bed. I look up at Tomás, and as soon as I'm getting ready to demand that they release me, I begin to feel it. Whatever Tomás injected into me is now taking effect.

I feel like I'm becoming lightheaded and weak. I'm getting the sensation that the room is spinning. I'm seeing circles, now multiple flashing colors: blue, red, and green like a rainbow. If I were standing up, I'd have to sit down, because no level of strength seems to flow through my body. The walls are moving in on me, and I can barely make out who Tomás or Dr. Mosley are. My eyes are heavy, and before I can take my next big breath, it's lights out for me.

CHAPTER THIRTY

I can hear voices around me: people talking. I recognize some of the voices, but I can't open my eyes to see who the individuals are. My eyes are very heavy, but I'm slowly getting them to open. I get them cracked enough to see Paul standing over my bed. He's smiling down at me. What is his problem? Why is he here? We're done, and I have nothing to say to him.

"Samantha, it's good to see you awake," Paul says. "Are you feeling ok?"

I'm feeling so drained, so heavy, that I'm *trying* to answer Paul, but I feel like I'm just mumbling. Nothing is coming out of my mouth; therefore, I nod my head yes to Paul. I can feel my eyes closing back, but I can still hear the conversations going on around me.

I hear someone say, "She was transferred here weeks ago. Her mom's sister had her moved because it was closer to where she lived."

My mom's sister...ok, so Aunt Robin knows I'm here. Where is she?

Then the other voice says, "It's a darn shame. Stress will do this to you...it's important to take care of your mental health, I feel sorry for her."

Who's she talking about? Who's she feeling sorry for? Not me, I hope. I'm doing very good, and I'll do much better if they'd just discharge me from this hospital.

I feel someone rubbing the back of my hand, but I can't open my eyes. *Who is it? Who's touching me? Paul, is that you? Is that Aunt Robin? Who is it...better yet, why am I so tired? What have they given me that I can't open my eyes?*

Then I feel some wet lips kiss the top of my forehead, and I hear Paul's voice.

"I told you, I promised."

As much as I can't stand Paul right now and as much as he has gotten on my nerves, I don't want him to leave. I need him to help me out of this. I need Paul at this very moment, but Paul is leaving. I can hear him gathering his stuff.

My thoughts are, *Nooo, Paul, don't go. Wait, I just need to rest. Once I get over this jetlag, I can open my eyes, and I'll be able to talk to you. Paul, please don't leave me here.*

I'm yelling internally, but nothing is projecting externally. It's as if I'm locked inside of a box where I can see out, but no one can see that I'm on the inside. I'm locked inside of myself, and I have no clue as to how to get out.

Paul and the person that he was talking to walk out. I can hear their voices getting farther away from me. I'm still not able to make out the identity of the individual that he's talking to or what they were saying. I am so tired; I have no strength; I need my mom; she would have gotten to the bottom of this. I must rest…I need to rest. I'll close my eyes and allow myself to doze back off into what seems to be more like a hypnotic trance than normal sleep. But when I awaken, I'll be stronger and more able to communicate with them.

I awaken from what seems to be a quick nap, but as I look over at the white digital clock hanging on the wall over the television, I realize that what felt like a quick nap was actually three hours of sleep. I can't believe I've been asleep that long. I sit up on the bed and realize that I'm no longer strapped down.

I begin to look around the room; something doesn't look right. The room…the room looks different. The room I was in was much smaller than this room. This room that I'm in is larger, but there's

COFFEE

nothing in here but this bed and the television. When did they move me, and was I that sleep that I can't recall?

I look over to my left and see a button on the wall that reads, *press for help*. Therefore, I press the button and a soft-toned, crazy-sounding voice on the other end says, "Hello, Ms. Samantha, how may we help you?"

"Uh, yeah, I think I'm in the wrong room. When did I get here?"

"Ms. Samantha, you're not in the wrong room. Just relax; the doctor will be in shortly to talk with you."

"How can I relax?" I yell.

"Ms. Samantha, there's no need to get upset." There's that crazy-sounding voice.

Why does she talk like that? Her voice is annoying me. "Can you come in here, please?"

"Sure, Ms. Samantha, I'll come visit you."

I sit and wait patiently on the Voice to come. The Voice is what I'll call her until I get to know her. Minutes later, I can hear what sounds like someone unlocking locks to the door. I'm thinking, *Was I locked in here?*

A person walks through the door. I look her up and down thinking that she doesn't look like what her voice sounds like. I didn't expect her to look like this. I was expecting a woman of small stature. This nurse has on gloves, and she's not wearing a name tag.

She then says, "The doctor sent me to check your vitals and administer you your meds, so I'm here to do just that."

I'm sitting there in shock, thinking, *This isn't the lady that was on the other end of the intercom. The other lady had a voice that was weird and different. This lady's voice is loud and deep. It's a bit strong…it goes along with her body.*

"Where is the lady that I was talking to?" I ask.

"Honey, I don't know who you spoke with. All I do is follow orders."

She hands me the pills and a cup and says, "Take it with your coffee."

I'm thinking, *Coffee?* I look over on my nightstand and notice that there's a cup of coffee sitting there. The lady then hands me a napkin and continues to stand there watching me. I look at her, and she's staring directly at me. She's looking at me like I've done something to her.

Therefore, I ask, "Are you going to watch me take my medicine?"

"Yes, I must make sure you take it."

"Ok, I will." I look around, and there's no water, so I ask, "Is there no water in here?"

"Just take it with your coffee, it'll be ok," she says to me.

COFFEE

I take the meds, but I say to her, "I'm shocked that they're giving me coffee."

"You must be someone special," she says as she keeps looking over at the door.

I ask if she is waiting on someone, and she shakes her head and says no. She then takes the coffee cup from me and walks toward the door.

I say, "I wasn't finished drinking the coffee."

She acts as if she doesn't hear me. She gets to the door, and before she opens it, I notice that she peeks out the door first before leaving as if she were in a hurry. I'm thinking, *Something isn't right with this nurse. She's a bit odd.* I can hear the door being locked on the other side. I jump up out of my bed and run to the door to attempt to open it. It's really locked, and it appears a bit heavy.

"Hello, hello, nurse?" I say as I'm beating on the door. "Is anyone out there?"

I continue to do this until I become fatigued. I go back and sit on the side of my bed, which is a bit low. I get up from the bed and notice that the bed is low because it's directly on the floor. There are no legs, and nothing can get under the bed. In fact, it's not a bed; it's only two large mattresses stacked on top of each other. Ok, I'm thinking, *Where the hell am I?*

I sit back on the bed, trying to gather my thoughts to understand what has transpired. I recall being in

Helsinki for the competition and being fooled...I'm not sure. Did I win? I don't know.

The tears begin to fall from my eyes. I'm saddened because I have no answers. Oh, how I wish I could just talk to Mom right now. I begin to think about all the good days that she and I had. I remember the last summer that I was home and the trips we took together. I remember Ms. P. and Mom sitting on the porch, laughing, and talking. I remember my aunt coming to visit. I'm remembering a lot of the past, but I can't remember the most recent stuff... like how did I get here?

I lay back on my bed, looking up at the ceiling. I'm staring into the light fixture thinking that my life has spiraled out of control. First, by losing Mom, being by her side while she was sick and watching her die in my arms. I begin to cry again just thinking about it. I was so mad at her for not telling me that she was sick. Why would she do that? She left me alone...she didn't give me a time to cope with it.

I grab the remote to turn the television on, and while it's coming on, the screen that pops up says *Homestead MI*. And I'm thinking, *Michigan?* When did I arrive in Michigan, and how did I get here?

CHAPTER THIRTY-ONE

The following day is long, and I'm still a bit confused. The nurse walks in and notices that my television is still on the introduction channel.

Therefore, she says to me, "Good morning, Ms. Samantha, how are you today?" She takes the remote and says, "Here you go sweetie."

She turns the channel, and I notice that everyone on it appears to look like everyone that I've met in Helsinki. What in the world is going on? The lady that's on this introduction channel looks exactly like Jax. I continue watching the show, which is about a designer school where people compete for a substantial amount of money.

The nurse turns to me and says, "This is your favorite reality show. You've been watching it every day since you've been in here."

"Every day since I've been here? Wait, how long have I been here?" I ask.

The nurse turns to me and says, "Well, honey, I've been your nurse for a pretty long time."

"Ok, but what is a long time?" I say to her.

She looks at me with a befuddled look and says, "Maybe you should speak with your doctor when he returns."

Flustered and agitated, I attempt to sit up in my bed, but I notice that I'm only allowed to sit up so far because I'm restrained once again with these brown-looking straps on my legs and arms.

"What are these?" I yell to the nurse.

"Ms. Samantha, those are for your own safety," she says. "Those are four-point restraints."

"I know what they are, but why in the hell am I being restrained again?" I begin to yell and scream, "Help, someone help me."

"Ms. Samantha—"

I interrupt her, "No, don't 'Ms. Samantha' me. Go get Doctor Whatever-the-hell-his-name-is immediately."

She turns hastily and walks out the door. What is going on? I'm thinking, *What did you do Samantha? Have you harmed someone?* I lean back into the trap of a bed that they have me in. The tears begin to flow. I *so* wish Mom were here right now. She would know what questions to ask, and she would tell them a thing or two. I wouldn't be in Michigan if I were sick. I would be home close to her. *Mom, I need you. I miss you so much.*

Yes, Mom would turn this hospital upside down.

The door of the room slightly opens. I can't see anyone, and then it closes back. I attempt to sit up again, forgetting that I'm tied down again like some sort of animal.

I holler out "Who is that? Doctor? Doctor, is that you?"

In walks a different nurse. She immediately says, "Samantha, I'm the head nurse, and I hear you have questions as to why you are here."

You're damn right I do. I say, "Here, where is *here*?"

"Here at Homestead. You're here at Homestead, and we've been taking good care of you. Now do you recall where you are, honey?"

I'm watching her like a hawk, noticing that her face is looking blurry. She at one point, looks normal, then her face appears like it's melting.

COFFEE

I go on to say, "First, stop calling me 'honey,' and no, I don't."

The word *honey* stuck out to me, and I remember what Mom used to say to me, "Samantha, you can get more flies with honey than vinegar. Be nice." Therefore, I adjust my tone, and I say to her, "Well, a little, but can you help me with a bit of clarity about Homestead?"

"Why sure dear. I must go handle my other patients, but I'll come back, and we'll talk. Is that ok?"

The heat in my body is now causing my blood pressure to rise, the wrath of anger gushes as I take a deep breath.

"Yes, yes, but can you please loosen these restraints from my arms and legs? They're hurting me, and I'm having anxiety knowing that they're there." I'm saying this while I'm looking at her badge and notice that her name is Erma.

Therefore, I say, "Ms. Erma?"

I allow the tears to start falling from my eyes. I put on the biggest water show that I can muster so that I can tap into what little humane side that she may have.

I ask, "Ms. Erma, is your mother still alive?"

Ms. Erma continues to do what she is doing, never looking at me. She says, "Yes, she is."

That's when I know I have to pour it on thick. "Well, my mother recently passed away, and I'm still grieving. And to wake up here in Homestead at a hospital in restraints, not knowing why, is overwhelming. I'm not going to hurt anyone, and I don't believe I have, so please take these off me."

Ms. Erma walks over to me and says, "Samantha, I know it feels weird to you, and you need answers. By now you should have gotten some, but I'm going to loosen your straps so that you can sit on the side of the bed. Would that help a little? But if you get out of hand again and start acting out, I will have you restrained again."

I shake my head yes, not understanding what she meant, but at this point, I really don't care. *Lady, just take these things from me*, is what I'm thinking.

Ms. Erma takes the straps from my legs first, and when she takes the first strap off, I immediately want to take the free leg and kick her in her ugly face, but I didn't. I smile and wait for her to release the second leg. Now she's loosening the right arm, and now my left. She turns to put the straps over in the chair. and my thoughts are wild.

I'm thinking, *As she turns, grab the back of her hair, and jam her head into the wall. Then as she falls, place the pillow over her head and suffocate her.*

These thoughts were wild, even too wild for me. I've never thought about harming anyone. I'm bothered by this…what's wrong with me? How could I think of something so violent to harm someone?

COFFEE

I sit on the side of the bed and decide to look out the room's one window. This window is very narrow and rectangular in shape. I walk over and peek out, and the view isn't what I expect. My view is of the front of the hospital, but majority of that view is of the parking lot. I see a few people being taken out in wheelchairs…I can't wait for that to be me. I wonder how long I'll be here.

As I continue to people watch, a van pulls up, and two men get out and open the van's side sliding door. They extend their hands, and I watch as a male steps out of the van but wait…this individual has something wrapped around him. I focus in more and notice that this man has on a white jacket that appears to be restraining him from moving his arms around. Then I realize…is that a…is that a strait jacket?

Oh my, why are they bringing him here? He needs to be in a mental institution if he's required to be in a strait jacket. I guess they like restraining people in this hospital. He probably didn't do anything wrong. These idiot nurses get scared when anyone raises their voices at them, and they want to restrain them just like they did to me. This is terrible. I can't wait to get out of here.

I continue to watch, and when he steps down out of the van, his feet are in shackles. The two men help him walk, and I notice as they walk him far enough in where I could see them from behind, on the back of their uniforms are the words *HOMESTEAD MI*

Interesting.

I'm thinking, *Oh, he's a prisoner and needs medical attention; that's why he's in shackles.* I pick up the remote control, turned on the television and switched back to the channel the nurse said I've apparently been watching for some time now.

I have so many questions with no answers. I'm in the hospital in Michigan, and I don't know how I got here. And I'm at the point where this hospital is restraining me. Did I have another episode? Surely, I couldn't have. Am I sick? I need to get to the bottom of what's going on.

I decide to watch this show all the way through. This episode is about a lady that was found in a dumpster behind an apartment, and it's looking as if the American girl has something to do with it. In this reality show, the main character is a dress designer from the United States, who's in Finland to compete, and it appears that everyone is against her. Everything seems the same, Vaughn is murdered, CJ is sneaky, and Paul is violent. This is just like what happened to me.

Did none of what I recall happen? Did I not go to Finland? If so, when did I get back into the States? I have questions, and I need answers. I turn the television off, and I try to think back to the day

COFFEE

I received the letter stating that I would be going to Helsinki, Finland. Then I start thinking about Mom and her sickness. I remember being there when she passed away. I recall taking her out every day and being by her side along with her nurse. I remember her funeral and the wonderful way people spoke about Mom. I recall waiting outside for the hospital to come and take her hospital bed and the items that they lent her while she was ill. I recall them showing up. I went into the house overwhelmed and crying out in deep grief.

I'm thinking about all of this, and the tears are now flowing again. My heart is so heavy from missing Mom. I love her so much. My life without her is nothing. It's like she was here, healthy, and doing well, and then in a blink of an eye, she became ill and was gone. Why, why, *why?* She didn't deserve this, and I don't deserve this.

I lie there in agony, and I just cry and cry. I decide to relax and take a nap. Tomorrow will be a better day, I'm sure of it, and I'll get the answers that I'm looking for.

CHAPTER THIRTY-TWO

I awaken, and I can hear voices at the door: one is female and the other is male. I wait for them to come into the room, but they're doing a lot of talking. Then the talking stops, and suddenly, in walks the nurse from the other day, but she's still not wearing a name tag.

She hands me a cup of coffee, but this time I say to her, "I didn't ask for any coffee, why are you bringing this to me? I didn't order any coffee."

She gives me a look as if she's trying to mother me as if to say, "drink the darn coffee." The look is so familiar, but when she extends her hand to me, I notice an odd-looking tattoo on the back of her

COFFEE

hand. I've seen this tattoo before: it's the same tattoo that was on someone else's hand. *Oh, why can't I remember where I saw it? Why is it like I have amnesia or something? I usually have a great memory, but lately my memory isn't there. I can't recall anything that's of any importance to me. I just need to rest, and maybe when I get all my energy back and get out of here, my memory will return.*

I politely take the coffee from her hand, and look up at her to say thank you.

She says, "Just like you like it."

"What do you mean, 'just like I like it'?" I say to her. "I don't usually drink coffee, and how would you know what I like?"

She takes a deep breath and provides me this warm smile, but there is something sadistic about her smile. I'm not sure what it is, but as I continue looking at her and trying to remember who it is that she reminds me of, she quickly turns her head away and my memory is triggered.

I remember! This lady…this nurse reminds me of Mom's nurse…I can't seem to think of her name…things are so foggy these days. My memory is gone, but I recall that she was so nice to Mom and me in mom's last days. I can't seem to remember much anymore, but I do recall how helpful she was in the end. Mom really liked her, and she trusted her as well, so much that Mom allowed her to fill out the power of attorney forms, the insurance, and all her medical paperwork and claims.

I was grateful because I was still wrapping my mind around Mom's sickness and why she hadn't informed me beforehand of her diagnosis. And there I was at the end of her terminal illness, losing valuable time with her.

The nurse reaches to take the cup of coffee from me, and I ask her, "What is the tattoo on the back of your hand?"

She covers the tattoo with her other hand, takes the cup from me, and quickly leaves the room.

CHAPTER THIRTY-THREE

Dr. Mosley walks into the room with a short fat white lady. She has short, curly hair, and she's wearing thick, black glasses. I don't know why, but her walk and talk make me want to watch the movie *Poltergeist*. And as she walks in right behind him, I'm thinking, *Not another nurse.*

"Ms. Samantha how are you today?" The doctor says.

"I would be great if someone would tell me why I'm here and why was I shackled like a psychopath."

"Oh, Ms. Samantha, that was not our intent to make you feel that way. We truly apologize but restraining you at that time was for your own good."

"I'm not so sure about that, but please tell me why I'm here."

"Absolutely, but first I would like to introduce you to Mrs. Haines. She's been assigned to you. She's here to help you sort through things."

Sort through things he says…the only thing needing sorted out is my date of release. That's what I wanted to say to him, but instead, I bite my tongue and say, "Ok, what is there to sort out?"

Dr. Mosley nods his head as if to say, "good, you are now becoming compliant."

He says, "What you have been through is very stressful, and we want to ensure that you're ok. Everyone around you is ok, and you're receiving the best therapy possible."

"Therapy!" I yell out. "I don't need any therapy."

"Of course, you don't feel you need it, Ms. Samantha, but in order for us to release you, there are certain requirements that must be met before we can sign off on you returning home."

Dr. Mosley and the lady pull a chair over to where I am and sit down right beside my bed. I'm listening to Dr. Mosley talk, but in my periphery, I can see the lady writing things down.

"Hey, hey, what are you writing about?" I say to her.

And with a high-pitched voice that doesn't match her stature, she says, "Oh, honey, no need to worry about what I'm doing; just answer the questions."

My thoughts are running wild as I am thinking, *Why do they think that I am their "honey?"* Therefore, I say to her, "Please don't call me that."

"As you wish," she says snarkily, as Dr. Mosely looks over at her as if to say "enough."

Dr. Mosely says, "Samantha, can you tell me everything that you can remember?"

"Unfortunately, Dr. Mosely, I don't recall much, and everything is weird around me; it's just weird. I woke up here, and the only thing that I remember is all the nurses coming in talking to me."

"'All the nurses' you say?"

"Yes, the one that comes in daily and that one who brought me coffee without me even asking."

"You had a nurse to bring you coffee? When did that take place, I didn't release you to drink coffee yet because of the caffeine."

"Yeah, the one with the tattoo. She seems familiar though, so maybe she's been in here before."

"No, no, there is only one nurse assigned to you, and that is Erma. I will check into it because we have particulars about too many people coming in and out of the patients' rooms."

"I don't see the problem; it wasn't like she was doing anything wrong. She just gave me coffee."

"I know it doesn't seem like a problem, but I still must look into who ordered the coffee and why.

COFFEE

However, thank you for informing me. So go on, tell me about you."

"Well, Doctor, as you know, my mother passed away and—"

Dr. Mosely interrupts me and says, "Your mother passed away? When did this happen?"

"Yes, Mom passed away right before I went to Helsinki to compete."

Dr. Mosley doesn't realize it, but I'm noticing him and his sidekick cutting eyes at each other when I answer their questions. I guess they don't believe anything I'm saying. Well, it goes both ways, because I don't trust any of them.

Dr. Mosley then says, "Hmm, tell me about your mom's death."

"Well, there's not much to tell. She had cancer, and she passed away. I came home from school to help and to spend time with her, but she...wait, wait, wait. I know...I can remember. I know where I've seen the tattoo that the nurse had before."

"What nurse?" Dr. Mosley ask.

"The nurse with the odd tattoo; she was my mother's nurse."

"So your mother had a nurse?"

"Yes, she had a live-in nurse that took care of her."

"Tell me more."

"She stayed with us until Mom passed away. She was nice, but she had a tattoo on her hand just like the nurse that gave me the coffee did. It looked odd to me then, and now it's funny, but the tattoo...the tattoo almost looked like a...a coffee bean."

"So, your mom had cancer, and had a nurse that lived with you all, and this nurse had an odd tattoo on her hand that looked like a coffee bean. And there was a nurse that came into your room and gave you coffee...coffee that you didn't order, and she also had that same tattoo? Is that what you're telling me."

"Yes, exactly. That's what I'm saying."

"Ok, Ms. Samantha, we've had enough for today," he says. "I'll administer your medication to you, and we'll be back to see you once the medication begins to work."

"Wait, what do you mean 'work'? Do you not believe me? Do you think I'm lying?"

"No, no, of course not, Ms. Samantha."

"Why would I lie to my doctor? And you haven't even told me why I'm here. What happened? I passed out in Helsinki but ended up here in Homestead hospital. Am I diabetic? Do I have cancer? What's wrong with me, doc?"

Dr. Mosley stands up and becks for the lady to come with him. They leave my room, and I can hear the two of them talking.

Mrs. Haines says, "I'll call her."

And I'm wondering, *Her, who? Who are they going to call?*

CHAPTER THIRTY-FOUR

The night seemed longer than any night that I can recall since being here. No one has told me how long I've been in the hospital, and I'm ready to go. I don't understand what's keeping me here under their observation. I can walk, I can talk, and I don't feel any pain. I have no monitors hooked to me; therefore, when the nurse comes back in my room, I'm going to tell her that I feel fine and that I'm checking myself out of this hospital.

"Good morning, Samantha, how are you feeling?" Nurse Erma says as she enters the room.

"I'm feeling pretty good. I'm glad to see you, Ms. Erma. I'm going to check myself out of here.

COFFEE

I haven't been told why I'm here. I have no pain, no nothing, and since nobody wants to tell me what happened when I passed out, I'm going home."

"Hmmm, we can't discharge you as of yet."

"Why? Why are you all keeping me here?"

"When Dr. Mosley or Mrs. Haines comes back into the room, ask them to explain everything to you."

"I will do that."

"Great," she says as she leaves.

What is going on? None of this makes sense. I wonder if I can call Ms. P.? Maybe she knows…she knows everything. I push the button for Erma to come.

"Hi, Ms. Samantha, can I help you?" says a voice over the intercom. "Erma, is that you?"

"Yes, it's Erma," she says. "Do you need anything?"

"Yes, can you please come. Erma comes into the room and says, "how may I help you?"

"I can't find my purse. Do you know where it is?"

"No, I can't say that I've seen it. Actually, when you were admitted, you didn't have anything with you but what you had on."

"What? I didn't have my purse with me? That doesn't make any sense. How did I get here, again?"

"I'm not sure how you arrived, but I do know that you didn't have anything, because we don't allow patients to bring anything with them when they arrive," says Erma.

"What kind of hospital is this? Most patients have their purses, keys, phones, or wallets, so they normally have something with them. Well, can I at least make a phone call?"

"Who will you be calling?"

"What business of yours is it to who I'll be calling? But if you must know, I want to call my neighbor, Ms. P."

"Ok, I will check with the doctor and see if that's allowed. If so, I'll bring a phone in here for you to place one call."

"One call? Is this jail?"

Erma gives me a look that I wasn't expecting.

"Erma, surely I'm not in jail, am I?"

"No, Samantha. It's just…many patients have referred to this place as being sort of like a jail, and I was thinking about how you're saying the same thing. Interesting. However, I'll check with Dr. Mosley, and if he says yes, I'll be back."

While waiting for Ms. Erma to come back, I decide to walk around the hospital. I open my room door and look out. I step out of my room, and as I'm walking down the corridor, I take notice that others are walking around as well. But they all seemed a bit spaced out, as if they're drugged up. There's a lady standing by a door; she's twisting her hair over and over and over. Then there's a man sitting in the middle of the corridor doing absolutely nothing.

COFFEE

As I continue to walk down this corridor with all the white walls, I notice the locks outside of all hospital room doors. I notice that all the patients, including myself, have on these white gowns. What is this place?

I make it to the end of the corridor, and I notice a sign that says *Café* with an arrow pointing towards another corridor, but I also notice that there's another door with an exit sign. I'm going to take my chances, walk out the door, and leave this mad house. I walk over to the door, and I push it: nothing. I push it again, and a very loud buzzer goes off.

Red lights above the door are flashing. The one man that was sitting in the corridor hops up and runs down the hall screaming. The lady twisting her hair begins to jump up and down, laughing and making some weird noises. I can hear banging on the doors by the patients that are in their rooms.

I look up and immediately, Erma and three other individuals are running toward me like they're about to tackle me on a football field. I step away, thinking they're running for someone else, but they run directly to me, grab me, and begin to drag me away from the door. I'm screaming, kicking, and yelling bloody murder. Erma calls for the head nurse, and a totally different nurse rushes in, grabs a syringe, sticks me in my arm, and…here we go again, lights out.

CHAPTER THIRTY-FIVE

I can hear someone talking at the door. I close my eyes so I can hear them better. I can hear the male voice asking what time she's expected to be here, and the lady says no later than 4:00 p.m. I look over at the clock on the wall, and it's 3:48 p.m. Whoever they're discussing will arrive any minute now. I'm praying it's someone that can answer all the many questions that I have.

I try to move my arms, and once again, I have been restrained like before. Why? Why are they doing this to me? As the tears begin to flow from my eyes and the many questions are floating around in my head, I'm beginning to feel helpless.

COFFEE

Erma walks in, and the look on her face is sorrowful. I ask if everything is ok, and she says, "I'm sorry Ms. Samantha, that we had to restrain you again, but I've got good news for you."

"I'm getting out of here?" I say to her excitedly.

"Not quite," she says, "but you will have your first visitor since being here for all these months." She says this as she grabs my chart and walks back out of the room.

I'm so excited to hear that I'm having a visitor that it doesn't immediately register that she said that I'd been here for "all these months." *Months,* I thought. How *many* months? And how is that possible?

As I'm sitting, awaiting my visitor, I can hear commotion outside of my door. The voice sounds familiar; I can only make out one sentence: "It's her daughter; she has the right."

Surely, that's not my visitor because no one would be saying that about me. My mom is gone… she's been gone almost a year now, and I'm still trying to adjust to losing her. Just when I think the commotion is settled, I hear a loud *bump* to my room door. I look over and see the wheels of a wheelchair entering in. I can simultaneously hear someone saying, "We are going in here, and you better not try to stop us."

I recognize the voice: it's *Ms. P*. And she's pushing a wheelchair. As I lift my head to see who's in the wheelchair, I get the biggest shock of my life, a shock that takes my breath away. Ms. P. is here, and she's pushing a person in the wheelchair, and that person is Mom!

Ms. P. burst into the room. She's giving the guards the blues, and they are backing off.

"Mom," I yell, in tears. I attempt to get out of the bed, but I'm still in restraints. "Mom, Mom, oh my God, how could this be? You're supposed to be… you were…I saw you…" I can't even get the words to come out of my mouth. "Mom, I even attended your funeral. What's going on?"

The thoughts immediately start racing through my head. *I'm really crazy as they have said. My mother isn't dead; she's alive. What's wrong with me?* The tears are flowing as I look Mom in the face. She appears very weak and feeble, but she's able to speak.

She says, "Sam, I am so sorry." And now the tears that were once a small trickle down her face are now streaming like a well-running river.

"Mom, you have nothing to be sorry for…but I thought you'd died. Am I going crazy?"

Mom looks up at me and says, "Sam, I assure you that you're not going crazy."

"But Mom, how can you be alive, when I recall watching you—"

"You watched me do what, Sam?" Mom says. "Yes, I've been sick, but what did you watch?"

"Mom, you died!"

COFFEE

"Died? What do you mean, died?" Ms. P. exclaimed. She's over in the corner crying in her Ms. P. fashion; she's melodramatic. "Sharon is more alive than ever before. Did this hospital tell you that your mom died? Who told you such foolishness?" Ms. P. keeps going on and on so much that Mom puts her hand up to Ms. P. to tell her to hush.

Mom says, "Samantha, baby, I don't know who told you I was dead, or why you would believe such, but I'm here baby. I'm weak, but I'm here."

My thoughts are running wild, *I can't quite understand what's taking place. Mom says I'm not crazy, but if I'm not, why did I think she was dead? I know I saw her body. I planned her funeral. I picked out her casket…saw all her family and friends. How can this be?*

I stare at Mom for a moment. I want to make sure that my mind is in the right place, that I'm seeing what I'm seeing. Ms. P. stops her crying and other shenanigans and comes over to the bed I'm shackled to.

She looks down at my restraints and says, "Oh Lord, they have this child in shackles; we got to get her out of these." She gets on her phone, and she calls someone and tells them that she's at the hospital. She says, "Oh yeah, we found her. She's in shackles like an animal. They didn't want to let us in here, but I got in. You knew I would…no, no, they haven't found that crazy Ms. Cox yet, but I reckon she'll slip up soon."

As Ms. P. is talking on the phone, she pushes Mom close enough to my bedside that we can hold hands.

"Mom, I'm confused. I don't know what's going on."

Just then, Erma walks into the room, and she says, "Ma'am, I'm going to release you from those restraints, but please don't do anything that would cause me to have to restrain you again."

I nod my head to show that I agree with what she's saying. At this point, I'll do or say anything to be released so that I can wrap my arms around my mother one more time. As soon as Erma releases my hands and feet, I leap up, rush over to Mom, and give her the biggest hug that I can muster up. My arms around Mom feel so good, but even while I hug her, I can feel her bones and the frailness of her body. Mom is weak. She's sick, but Mom is alive, and I want to scream it to the top of my voice. My mom is alive!

Once Mom and I finish our little family reunion, I say to her, "Mom, what's going on? Do you know why I'm here? I don't feel sick. All I did was pass out, right?"

Mom with her weakened voice, lowers her head and says, "Ms. Cox…it was Ms. Cox, Sam."

COFFEE

"Ms. Cox?" I ask, "what does she have to do with me getting sick in Finland and being here?"

Just as I'm making my statement, Ms. P. screams out with a squeaky-like voice and says, "Oh Lord, this girl thinks that she was in Finland. They've messed her all up."

Ms. P. is behaving worse than she's ever behaved before. She's very animated and extra, flailing her hands in the air. Mom finally tells her to calm down.

Mom then looks over at me and says, "I'm sorry that I trusted her, Samantha. She took us for everything: the medications that she gave me weren't to help me. Instead, she was poisoning me and making me sicker than I really was. She was also poisoning you. And after you started hallucinating, she knew the right things to say to trigger you to act out. She had you committed to this mental institution, and she thought that I would die after she poisoned me. But I didn't die. And during that time of her being at the house, she placed drugs in your coffee and had you drinking it, thinking it was my special coffee, but it was actually making you have psychotic episodes."

"Mom, I don't remember any of this. How could she have done that? And you said she took everything. How did she take everything, Mom? How?"

"Samantha, have a seat," says Ms. P. "Your momma has a lot to explain."

Mom looks up at me and drops her head back down just as quickly as she lifted it. She places her hand on her forehead and begins to cry again.

She says, "Once she had my trust, I allowed her to fill out a lot of forms that she stated I would need. I had no idea that the forms were giving her power of attorney over me. And once she had control, her next task was to get you out of the way, and she did that by drugging you, this way she could prove that you were incompetent."

"But Mom, I'm not incompetent by far."

"I know, babe, but with all the drugs in your system, you were telling people that you had traveled to Helsinki for some fashion competition, and while there, you said people were murdered. You even were saying that people were following you and had kidnapped you. You were talking very crazy and wouldn't listen. You were telling people that some guy named CJ, which is the guy from the hospital, was the one doing the killing and set you up so that his sister could win the fashion competition. And when the police came to talk to you, you attacked them and ran away."

"I did what?"

"Yes, babe, you attacked the police, ran off, and ended up in the hospital. Then somehow, the hospital transferred you out. Samantha, we were being told what was taking place, but every time we would

COFFEE

try to get to where you were, you would have another episode and run away. We had no idea where you were, and no one had heard from you. I'm sorry…it's all my fault. Please forgive me." Mom is saying this while her breathing has become heavy.

She's getting overwhelmed; Mom can't breathe!

Ms. P. immediately runs out and hollers for the nurse to come in. Erma rushes in and sees that Mom is breathing heavily. She calls over to the nurses' station and tells them to bring the oxygen. While we're waiting on the nurse with the oxygen, Erma is trying to calm Mom down. She's telling her to take deep breaths in and to let it out slowly. She has Mom to do this a few times until another nurse comes in. They place the oxygen apparatus over Mom's nose and mouth, Mom takes a few breaths, and she's now breathing much better.

I'm rubbing Mom's back as I am talking to her, "Mom don't apologize, we'll discuss it later. Save your strength; I need you to get better."

"You understand Sam, right?"

"No, I don't understand, but we'll talk later."

"No, no, no. I must explain it now, Sam, I must."

"Mom, no, it's ok."

Mom looks over at me. She's shaking her head and pointing to her purse. While digging through her purse, in a very weak voice she says, "Ms. Cox conspired with her friend and Paul, and between the two of them, they were able to get papers drawn up to steal the house away from us. She was doing this while I would be sleep due to my medications or when you would be taking me for a walk."

Mom is able to get that much out, but Ms. P. has to finish what Mom was trying to say. Ms. P. explains it all. She shared that it was during that time when Ms. Cox was able to find Mom's important documents, she had them drawn up with her as the sole beneficiary. And by drugging me, she was able to say that I was mentally incapable of caring for myself. She even had Paul and a few others write letters to confirm what she was saying. Paul did this just to get back at me. She would have me meet her in public places, and we would drink some of Mom's special coffee. Ms. P. says it was during those times that I would act out and become irate, and because this was in public, I had no idea that I was helping to build her case against me.

I don't recall any of the instances, but I do remember Ms. Cox telling me that I was grieving. I remember being in a café and having conversations with people.

Ms. P. then says, "You never went to a café, Sam. At first, you were allowed to walk down to your therapist's area, it was across from the cafeteria. You and your therapist Eevi would sometimes go sit in the cafeteria to talk. She was good for you."

"Eevi, I remember her, but I don't remember seeing a therapist at all."

"You don't?" Says Ms. P. "You would meet with her every Tuesday. We were told that it was working, but then you started not wanting to go."

"How do you know all of this if you all didn't know where I was?"

"Once we found out, we had to go through the courts just to see you, chile. It was like pulling teeth just to get this one visit, but we wanted to make sure everything was in order before coming up here."

"Wow, so Ms. Cox had this set up perfectly enough that every time I behaved in this manner, someone was documenting it. Ms. Cox was a snake all along, and Paul was a bitter boy who couldn't accept rejection. Unfortunately, Mom, in her state, had no idea as to what she was signing, but she trusted Ms. Cox."

Ms. P. says, "Yes, girl, that woman was a mess, and she took advantage of Sharon. It was good that Sharon was hospitalized because that's when the doctors were able to see that the medications Sharon was prescribed was not in her system. They were wondering why it wasn't working, so they ran more tests and found other medications in her system that she wasn't prescribed. And they were causing her to be sick. We know it was that Cox lady because she was the one administering Sharon's medications to her."

I'm listening to what Ms. P. is telling me, and it all sounds so bizarre.

I say to Ms. P. "This is really crazy, like in a movie."

Ms. P. says, "Yes, girl, your mom said y'all was in the kitchen, and Sharon handed you her coffee to drink. And the next thing she knew, she was in the hospital, and you were gone. Nobody knew where you were. It was like you just disappeared."

Mom looks at me and says, "But we have you now. We're going to get you out of here, but don't eat or drink anything that they provide you. I don't want anything clashing with whatever Ms. Cox has been giving you."

Ms. P. finally gets herself together and she begins to tell us about the lawyer that will be helping with our case. She says, "I never liked that Ms. Cox lady. I knew she was up to no good. Nobody knows where she's at, and a few days ago, she sold y'all's home."

"She sold our home? Are you kidding me? Then, Mom, where are you staying?"

Mom's head is hanging over, but she lifts her finger and points in Ms. P.'s direction.

"Ms. P. has come through again and allowed me to stay with her until I'm strong enough to care for myself. Then I'm going to go stay with your Aunt Robin. I just wanted to find you first."

"I wish the police could find that wretched woman and put her away," says Ms. P.

COFFEE

I sit there listening to Ms. P. going on and on about what had transpired, and the more she talked, the more my memory seems to want to come back. It doesn't come back all at once, but enough memories return to recall that Paul came to visit me, at least I think he did, someone needs to check into that, and there was a lady, a nurse that came here to my room. Even Dr. Mosley stated he didn't know who she was, but I recall that she looked familiar. There was something about her...I wonder if that was her?

I look over at Ms. P. and Mom talking, and I interrupt their conversation and ask, "Do either of you recall if Ms. Cox had a tattoo on her hand?"

Mom held her head up as if she were thinking, but Ms. P. blurted out, "Hell yeah, she did. Looked like a dookie turd, right?"

I give Ms. P. a laugh. I expect nothing less of her.

I say, "I'm not sure what it was. It actually looked like a coffee bean, but do you recall that?"

"Of course, I do. I always wondered what it was, and she would never give a straight answer."

I beck for Ms. P. to come closer. Mom appears to have dozed off to sleep; she even looks relaxed during all this mess. I don't want to stress her out, especially now that I have her back.

I say to Ms. P., "There's a lady that came to my room; she stated she was the head nurse for this hospital, but Dr. Mosley said that he didn't know who she is. Ms. P., she looked very familiar to me: it was something about her. But she also provided me with a cup of coffee that I didn't ask for—"

Ms. P. jumps back so fast that she bumps against Mom's wheelchair, startling her.

She then says, "Coffee? Did you drink it? Oh Lord, that was how she was drugging you last time. You didn't learn, girl. I'm calling the investigator right now."

Mom sits up, looks over at us, and says, "What? Who are y'all talking about? What's going on?"

And before I can tell Ms. P. not to say anything, she says, "Sharon, Samantha thinks she saw Ms. Cox up here. She said she even gave her some coffee."

Just as Ms. P. is telling Mom everything that I'd said, a small group walks into my room: Dr. Mosley, the investigator, and Mrs. Haines. Erma is following behind them, and she immediately comes over to me and begins to take my vitals.

"Ms. Scott," says Dr. Mosley.

Mom and I both reply, "Yes?"

Dr. Mosley chuckles and says, "Ms. Samantha Scott, I'm so sorry that you were sent here and held under false pretenses. We were able to run your blood sample, and we were able to verify that you've been under a drug-induced psychosis."

"So the drugs I were given...will they cause any side effects?"

"That's very possible," he says, "but it was a combination of so many different drugs, that we'll have to transfer you to Ball Memorial to detox you and get a better understanding of what drugs you were given."

"I don't need to detox; I am fine right now as I am,"

"Yes, you are correct, but you're also on antipsychotic medications that are controlling you. Once those run out of your system, you will react."

"No. No more hospitals." I say this as my once-joyous spirit has now been crushed by the thought of leaving Mom's side. I don't want us separated; I want her right beside me at all times. Dr. Mosley ushers Mom and the others out of the room, leaving me with Erma.

I look over at Erma and ask, "Why can't I just be detoxed, here?"

Erma takes me by the hand and says, "Ms. Samantha, you really don't know where you are?"

I pull my hand away and say, "Yes, I do. I'm in the hospital in Homestead, Michigan. I saw the back of one of the orderlies' uniforms, and it said *Homestead MI*."

Erma looks at me and shakes her head, she says, "No, Ms. Samantha, you aren't in Michigan. You are in Homestead, and the *MI* stands for *mental institution*, not Michigan. You're in Homestead Mental Institution.

CHAPTER THIRTY-SIX

Court is in Session

"All rise; the Honorable Marilynn Prism is presiding," says this middle-aged white guy. He's the bailiff standing over by the door. He seems so frail, so much so that I can't imagine him being able to tackle anyone if the need arises. But I guess he doesn't need to, as long as he has that gun hanging on the side of his pants. The gun is so heavy that it's causing his pants to droop a little…poor, skinny guy.

In walks this beautiful-looking black woman in a black robe. She's well-manicured, her hair is very long, her make-up is superb, and even though she doesn't have her nails painted, I can tell that she had a very expensive manicure. She walks up to the desk, and before she sits down, she says to everyone, "You may take your seats."

Mom is in her wheelchair, off to the side because there's no area for her to sit up near us. But Ms. P., Dr. Mosley, Mrs. Haines, and a Homestead representative are all here. They're joined by an attorney that Ms. P. hired to help us with our home and to have me properly released. And Erma was here too, even though she sat all the way in the back.

The attorney then calls Dr. Mosley to the stand, after being sworn in, the attorney tells Dr. Mosley to explain the situation of Ms. Samantha Scott.

Dr. Mosley has a black briefcase with him, and he begins by pulling out a stack of papers and placing them on the podium.

He says, "Your Honor, I have been treating Ms. Samantha for nearly six months, and I must admit, she has been nothing but trouble since the first day she arrived. I'm not aware of this conspiracy with one of the hospital staff or anyone else that colluded together to have her falsely committed."

When Dr. Mosley says this, Ms. P. stands up and hollers then falls back as if she had fainted. Others are shocked, and I'm confused. What is he doing? Why is he saying that?

"Order in the court, order in the court," Judge Prism yells as she bangs her gavel. "Dr. Mosley, are you standing in my court stating that Ms. Scott truly suffers from mental illnesses? Because I've read your initial report and what you are saying now doesn't coincide to what you've previously wrote. Therefore, I need answers, does Ms. Scott suffer from mental illnesses?"

"What I am saying is—"

Judge Prism interrupts Dr. Mosley and says, "No, answer the question, Dr. Mosley."

Dr. Mosley gets quiet, and he looks toward the back of the court room. Ms. P. notices Dr. Mosley constantly turning around looking toward the back; therefore, she looks back to see who he is looking at. It's none other than Ms. Cox.

Dr. Mosley is looking terrified. He then swallows and says, "Your Honor, can I take a break?"

"No, you may not. What you can do is answer this simple question: are you stating that Ms. Scott is mentally incapable of caring for herself?"

At this time, Ms. P. slowly walks toward the back of the room, and Ms. Cox is so focused on Dr. Mosley that she doesn't see Ms. P. coming toward her.

"Dr. Mosley, this is my last time asking you. You are either going to answer me, or I'm going to find you in contempt of court."

COFFEE

Dr. Mosley is still looking back, but as he turns back toward the judge, there's a loud banging and screaming in the back of the room.

Judge Prism begins to bang her gavel repeatedly. "Order in the court, order in the court."

I look back to see what the commotion is, and I see that Ms. P. has grabbed Ms. Cox by the neck and has thrown her to the floor. The guards that were standing outside of the courtroom rush in and grab Ms. P.

Just when Ms. Cox stands up and is getting ready to leave the courtroom, in walk two big police officers. They block her from leaving and place her in handcuffs.

Mrs. Haines quickly walks to the back of the courtroom. She then takes her badge from around her neck and says, "Ms. Vernita Coffée a.k.a. Ms. Cox, you are under arrest for fraud, money laundering, identity theft, conspiracy, and a whole list of other things. Lady, we have caught you, and we've been waiting four years to catch you."

It all happened so fast. Ms. Cox was on her way to jail, and what we didn't know was that Mrs. Haines was an undercover FBI agent that had been watching Ms. Cox closely. She'd finally tracked Ms. Cox to Homestead. Apparently, Ms. Cox had done this before in several other states, but the individuals passed away and the FBI could never find her.

They would get close but never enough to arrest her. Ms. Cox was so clever that right before court she threatened Dr. Mosley, and he was scared to testify on my behalf. She had convinced Paul to say that I was going crazy and even made a way for him to come to the hospital to visit me without anyone knowing.

Ms. P. says in a loud voice, "Four years? It took me only a few months to find her. I need y'all's job."

Judge Prism hits her gavel and says to Dr. Mosley, "Sir, are you ready to answer the question now?"

Dr. Mosley stands up, this time with confidence, and says, "It is through my expertise as a medical professional that Ms. Samantha Scott is mentally sound, and any disruption in her mental stability was due to her being placed in a drug-induced psychosis. It is in Ms. Samantha Scott's best interest to be released."

Ms. P. yells out, "Yes, it's about time."

Judge Prism goes on to say, "The courts have read the documents at hand and listened to the testimony of Dr. Mosley and have found that Ms. Scott should be released immediately on her own recognizance."

The judge then stands up, turns directly toward me, and says, "Ms. Samantha Scott, on behalf of the court and myself, I'm sorry that you had to endure such traumatic experience for such a time. Please accept the apology of the court and go in good health. Court is dismissed."

COFFEE

She bangs her gavel but immediately turns around and says, "Bailiff, please take Dr. Mosley into custody as well." And she walks away.

Everyone is cheering and celebrating. Erma walks up to me and extends her hand for me to shake. She says, "I'm so sorry that you had to endure this. I ask that you forgive me; I had no idea."

I accept her apology, but instead of shaking her hand, I reach in and hug her.

Ms. P. runs over to where Mom is sitting in her wheelchair, "Sharon, Sharon, your baby girl is going home."

I'm walking toward Mom and Ms. P., and I hear Ms. P. say again, "Sharon, did you hear me? Your baby girl is coming home; it's all over."

Mom didn't respond, as I made my way over to them a feeling of emptiness quickly engulfs me, and the tears began to flow. And before I even look in Mom's face, I already know that Mom is at peace, and this time, Mom is really gone.

EPILOGUE

Mom and I made the hugest mistake in trusting Ms. Vernita Coffée Cox, but we were at a desperate time in our lives. We had just been faced with knowing that at some point our friendship, our sisterhood, and our long-lasting mother-daughter relationship would soon be a simple vapor with a myriad of memories.

It's the nature of life. It's something that we all know will one day take place, but we don't like to discuss it. Death, we don't like to think about it, death, and we surely don't want it to knock at our doors. Why? Because it's death: an action where the beginning and the end shows up together and leave as one.

COFFEE

Mom was not elderly: she was young. She wasn't a smoker or a drinker, but cancer crept in and invaded her space. Her being the woman that she was, she never wanted me to have to take care of her. She never wanted to be a burden to me, and when we would have these conversations, I would always tell her, "Mom, you are never a burden and will never be one. It would be my honor to care for you if you need."

Mom was a proud, independent woman, and when the time came, I can only imagine the thoughts that ran through her mind.

Ms. P., there is a lot that I can say about her; however, I must admit that Ms. P. loved Mom. She was truly her friend and truly there for her. In the end, Ms. P. is alright in my book.

During Mom's preparation time for her funeral, it was funny because it was almost like how I recalled it during my psychotic episode. The way Mom was dressed and the flowers around and on top of her casket were all the same. It was as if I had seen everything in the future but believed it was happening in the now. The only difference was, Mom had never gone to the church where the funeral was being held. Instead, Aunt Robin came in and handled pretty much everything, and the funeral was at her church, and her pastor eulogized Mom. He had met Mom, stopped by the house on many occasions to pray for Mom, and from there, Mom would watch their church services online and pay tithes. Mom's doing so caught the interest of Ms. P., and they both would sit in the house and watch church together.

When Aunt Robin found out what Ms. Cox had done, she took every cent that she had and helped Mom obtain an attorney so that she could get her back on her feet and get our home back. In the end, we got our home back, but it'll never be the same because Mom's presence will no longer grace it. Now *that's* a memory that didn't change: the hurt, the pain, the feeling left behind. It wasn't a myth or the drugs talking; it was a true feeling, a feeling that swept me away back then and opened me up to needing help in the first place.

Ms. Cox, I honestly thought she was kind and compassionate at first, but I now see that she used her influence, wits, and the trust of her patients and their family members to take advantage of them. She hung around long enough showing compassion and concern—not only to the patient but also to the family—and doing so gave her leverage with us. We trusted her. She acted as if she cared for Mom's wellbeing, not just her health. And overall, I trusted her. I fell for it because I needed to. I needed to have someone that could help me handle the situation that I was facing. I was preparing myself to grieve, but instead of allowing Ms. P. and Aunt Robin in,

COFFEE

I shook hands with the devil, and it almost cost me my life. It did cost me time, time with Mom that I can never get back. But because of her behavior, Ms. Cox will get all the time that I and others lost while she's locked up in jail.

And that Paul, Paul was a creep and still is, Paul is a narcissist that was mad because I broke up with him, therefore he too shook hands with the devil to get back at me. Little does he know that what goes around, comes back around.

As for me, I'm ok. I have a bit of memory fog on some things, but for the most part, I'm doing well. I've gone back to school, and I had a meeting with Ms. Voltsclaw. To my surprise, I found out that I really was accepted to study abroad. Ms. Voltsclaw had put me in for a designer's competition, and I was accepted, but it wasn't in Helsinki. I've never been to Helsinki…I guess it was my desire but never my reality. The reality is, all the running and trying to escape the police was my running within Homestead from the doctors and trying to avoid being locked up. Homestead was my Helsinki. Ms. Cox did a whammy on me when it came to my mental state and our finances. I'm just happy to know that no one really died, I imagined all of this. Everyone I met in my psychotic state, I really met, but they all worked in the hospital. The drugs and Ms. Cox were what really took me on a trip to Helsinki, but it was all in my head.

The doctors have told me that I must take it easy because I was given so many drugs. They said I must be careful, making certain that I take my medications correctly. The medications that I am taking are constantly countering the drugs that are still in my system and any harsh effects they may have caused. I was also told that too much stress can trigger a nervous breakdown again, so I must take caution in monitoring the stress in my life.

I feel so terrible because I fell for Ms. Cox's foolishness. Because of her we almost lost the house. We were able to get it back, but Aunt Robin and, of course, Ms. P. and I are back and forth in court, trying to get the life insurance money that Ms. Cox swindled me out of when she faked Mom's death. Apparently, she had someone to create a fake death certificate, and by doing so, she took it all...*so* much that when Mom passed away, Aunt Robin had to pay for her funeral services because there was no policy.

The insurance company has been helpful in that they're going after Ms. Cox. They have filed charges and are attempting to recover every penny that was given to her. They informed me that it would take a long time because Ms. Cox has no income, no estate, or anything that they can use to retrieve restitution. The insurance company is trying to sell all her assets that were confiscated. Once sold, the money would be returned to them, and they would, in turn, return the money to me, knowing that it would not be enough...but it would be a start. Their greatest hope is finding her accomplice. Apparently, the reason she was able to get the papers changed so easily was because she had someone working on the inside as an insurance agent and had someone working at the vital statistics office, which handles the death records of individuals in the county. The investigators haven't been successful in tracking either of these individuals, so that has become a huge problem for everyone.

One good thing is the designer's competition is in France. Yes, I'll be traveling to France. It won't be for a year; it's only for six months. I'm very excited about the trip, but I question myself if this is too much and too soon. Aunt Robin will be traveling with me to make sure that I am ok. I'm staying with her, and she's helping me with the sale of the home. If we get the asking price, that money will be used to repay her for paying for Mom's funeral services. I will pay the investigators, give Ms. P. something for caring for Mom, although I'm sure she won't take it. But I *will* offer it, and in the end, whatever is left, I pray it's enough to get an apartment close to school. Aunt Robin has given me several real estate agents to call, and I've set up a meeting with Ms. Grace today. She has me meeting her at a coffee shop that's on the other side of town. Aunt Robin has even allowed me to use her car to make the drive.

I arrive at the coffee shop, and I sit near a window. I'm looking out the window, and everything feels so familiar to me. I'm reminiscing about everything that has transpired in my head, but I'm also grateful that I may have the opportunity of a lifetime to study abroad. As I'm sitting, I see an older woman walk into the coffee shop. She walks over to me and extends her hand.

She says to me, "Hello, Samantha."

I look up at her and say, "Ms. Grace?"

Ms. Grace nods her head and says, "Yes, that would be me." And she takes a seat across from me.

Ms. Grace and I sit there for at least two hours talking and discussing the sale of the house. The waitress would come over and ask if we wanted anything to eat or drink, and Ms. Grace would say, "Give us a few more minutes, please."

It seemed like the waitress had gotten tired of coming back to the table; therefore, she never returned to take our order. She disappeared until the time her shift was over because I saw her take her apron off and walk out the door.

Ms. Grace and I kept talking. She talked, I listened; I talked, she listened. She laughed, and I laughed, and we seemed to hit it off so well. Aunt Robin assured me that she hadn't spoken to Ms. Grace about what happened, and I didn't feel the need to either. I wanted the conversation to flow freely without her feeling the need to show sympathy or empathy toward me or the situation.

Ms. Grace is not married and doesn't have any children of her own, but she shared with me that she now will be raising three children—two nieces and a nephew—because her sister has recently been incarcerated. She didn't say what happened, just that her sister made some very bad choices and would be in jail for a very long time.

As we continue to become acquainted with one another and wrap up, Ms. Grace asks if I have any questions. I pause for a moment to think, and I say to her "No, I think you've given me everything that I need."

She finishes packing up all the information that was laid out on the table for me. She then stands up and says, "Samantha, I look forward to working with you."

At this time, I stand up, shake her hand, and say, "So do I, Ms. Grace, so do I."

As Ms. Grace is about to walk away, she turns back toward me and says, "Samantha, you can call me Eevi." She then turns around and walks out the door.

I sit down. I'm a bit shaken and almost out of breath. I'm trying to assure myself that everything is ok.

"It's ok, it's ok, Sam," I keep saying to myself.

You're not having another breakdown...you're ok. Many people have that name. I look down at the business card that she had given me and the name on it says, Ms. Eevi Grace. I continue to just sit, thinking, and trying to convince myself that everything was ok. I reach into my purse, searching for the card Aunt Robin gave me from her pastor. She says he does counseling. I think scheduling an appointment with him might help me in my healing. I feel ok, and I know things are going well, but just having someone to talk to wouldn't hurt.

As I continue to look for the card, the new waitress for my table walks up and asks, "Would you like a cup of coffee?"

I immediately turn toward her, give her a faint smile with a chuckle on the side and say, "No, a glass of water please."

Turn the page for an exclusive look at Rachel L. Sanders's new novel, a sequel to *Deceit on Dorchester*: THE CIRCLE OF DECEIT.

Coming in December 2023 by **Palmetto** Books

THE CIRCLE OF DECEIT

9:26 p.m.

The room was dark and still. No one moved or said anything after hearing what sounded like a gunshot. The storm had knocked the lights out. Visibility was null, and everyone was on high alert.

A voice from over in the corner hollers, "Is everyone ok? Is everyone accounted for?"

Another voice says, "Who's asking?"

And the reply was, "What difference does it make? Are you ok? And whoever picked the gun up from the table has to be the one who shot the gun."

Then this one heavy-toned voice that everyone recognized as being Officer Veeto says, "Calm down, calm down, everyone. Nobody panic, maybe it was a transformer that blew; we don't know if it was a gunshot."

Most of the people in the room began to agree with Officer Veeto, as he went on to ask, "Is the librarian still here in the room? Maybe she can direct us to where the circuit breaker is so we can try to get some light."

"No, she left earlier and told me to text her once we left so that she could lock the doors and set the alarm," says someone sitting over to the right. "She didn't need to be here to do that."

Just when the voice made that statement, Alicia's mom said, "If everyone would turn on their cell phone flashlights, it'll be enough to illuminate the room."

"Good idea," many began to say.

"But where can I find the flashlight on my phone?" Someone asked.

Alicia's mom said, "For those that can't find your flashlight on your phone, just open the phone so that the light will shine, and if you lift it, that will help."

The people began to find their flashlights, and those that didn't just opened their phones and lifted them. The room was illuminated enough to get a view of who was in the room. Then out of nowhere, there came a scream.

"It sounds like…it sounds like it's coming from near the doorway," Alicia's mom yells, as everyone pointed their lights toward the doorway.

Mrs. Beckwith screamed, "There's blood everywhere."

Everyone's attention and lights turned toward where Mrs. Beckwith was pointing and screaming. We all noticed the blood: there was a trail of blood leading out of the library door. It appeared to be trailing out toward the parking lot, but with all the rain that was coming down, the blood trail out there was quickly washing away.

"So it appears that someone has been hurt," someone said.

"More likely shot," another said.

Officer Veeto raised his hand and said, "We don't know. We don't know what has happened. We don't know anything; all we know for a fact is that the lights went out, we heard a loud sound—like a transformer blowing or a gunshot—and when the lights came back on, we heard a scream and saw something that appeared to be blood. Let's stop with the speculations, please!"

Mrs. Beckwith was overwhelmed but gathered up enough strength to say to Officer Veeto with a satirical and brashly tone, 'Like a gunshot' you say, and 'something that appears to be blood'? Are you drunk, crazy, or both? Isn't that enough? A gunshot and blood equals someone being shot. Wouldn't you all agree? It doesn't take a rocket scientist to believe that. You even agreed, so please don't treat us like children; tell us what is going on."

Before Officer Veeto could open his mouth, the guy from all the way in the back said, "How is he supposed to know more than us when he was here with us? How stupid can you be?"

Alicia's Mom chimed in with, "Right, he was right here all along."

Mrs. Beckwith took a napkin from the table where the snacks were sitting and awaiting to be devoured. She then wiped her face, cleared her throat, and said to the guy, "For one, he's the darn po-po; he should know. And two, I don't know who you are, or who you think you are, but if you call me stupid one more time, we'll be following a trail of blood to *your* body somewhere."

Officer Veeto was on his radio calling for backup while trying to keep everyone calm, but the look on his face was an indicator that this was far from calm and far from being over.

He tried to manage everyone, so he said, "Everyone, please go home. My team is on their way, and we will get to the bottom of this."

The mumbles and grumbles started as everyone slowly walked out of the library door into a night that one would never forget. The night was growing old, the rain was at a steady pace, and the people were frightened and confused, but no one shared their feelings. This simple community meeting may have just become a community murder, and we didn't know who the suspect was or who the victim was…if there was one. All we knew was, that something had taken place, and there was chaos on the horizon. Fear was setting in, and the residents of Seventy-Sixth and Dorchester were experiencing a calamity that could once again have shaken us to our core.

THE CIRCLE OF DECEIT

9:34 p.m.

The banging and loud chatter awakened me from my sleep. I could hear people talking and gasping, but I couldn't make out what was taking place. I threw my robe on and went to the window, but the rain had my window so misty that I couldn't see clearly. I could tell that there was a group of people that appeared to be standing in the street, but that was all I was able to make out. Therefore, I slipped my feet into my slippers and headed down the stairs. I got to my living room window with the hope of getting a better view, but the bushes in my yard had grown so tall in this past year that they had now blocked me from seeing further down the street. I remind myself that I must get these bushes cut down.

I opened the door to stand on my front porch, and as soon as I stepped out, Ms. Beverly from way down the street had made it to see what was going on. Ms. Beverly doesn't even reside on our block, but I guess with all the commotion, she wanted to know what was taking place, even if it meant walking down in the rain. Ms. Beverly was walking fast, and she had nothing covering her from the rain but a hat on her head.

When she got even with where I was, she yelled out to me, "They called me saying that there's a body in the middle of the street down here."

I guess the guilt of walking all the way down here in the rain when she has never walked down here before had convicted her, so she wanted to provide me with an explanation.

I said to her, "A body? Who is it, and who are they?"

"No one can tell," she said. "Grab your umbrella, girl, and come on, let's go and see."

I really didn't know Ms. Beverly; I've had a few conversations with her in passing, but truth be told, I wanted to know what was taking place as well. I tightened my robe around me, stepped into the foyer, grabbed my umbrella, and made my way down to the end of the street. This way was down in front of where the Blake house is. No one usually went to that end of the block…well, no one from around here. Ever since what happened with those nutty girls Felicia and Charnetta, it's like we've all tried to avoid that end of the block…but it's pretty hard to do that right now when you have a body lying in the street in the rain.

I wondered if they were just drunk and the "they" that called Ms. Beverly were exaggerating about the person being dead. I also wondered how the new neighbor, Ms. Carr, feels with all this taking place in front of her home.

I made my final approach toward the crowd, and in my periphery, I could see someone standing between the Blake house and Ms. Carr's house. But I didn't look over or turn my head in that direction; instead, I continued to walk until I met with the crowd.

9:41 p.m.

The streetlight from the end of the block wasn't bright enough for anyone to see. The misty rain that trickled down exacerbated the lack of visibility. The only thing that could be seen was a body in the middle of the street. How it got there was the million-dollar question, and what happened to this person, no one could answer. The only thing that stood out was that this individual wore blue jeans and red tennis shoes. The shirt was of a dark color, but no one could be sure because between blood and rain, its true color had been distorted.

Visibility was at a minimum, so much that no one could make out whether the body was a female or male, but suddenly someone from the back of the crowd yelled out, "It's Kelly."

"Kelly," everyone repeated as they looked around to see who had made that statement.

But the rain had become aggressive, and it was now providing a steady flow, blinding the eyes of everyone. However, many of them gasped, but there was one individual that blurted out, "How do you know that it's Kelly?"

And the murmurs of the crowd agreed with the question until the voice from the back said, "I saw her running earlier, and she had similar color clothing on."

The statement that the remains could be Kelly's shook those standing by. At first, it was a quiet scene, but now the chatter was growing so much that it began to drown out the sounds of the crickets.

"Kelly who?" one lady says.

"Oh well," another says, "if it *is* her, then."

"Then what?" says this unknown figure that was standing in the back.

With the help of the moonlight, we could see that this person had started walking toward where the crowd of people were standing. Many of them were outside in their coats with pajamas on under them. Several just had their robes on with umbrellas over their heads to keep them from getting wet. Then there were the braves ones who didn't care. Everyone was in this rain, and no one was making notice of the rain, as if the rain didn't exist. These people took the darkness and falling rain onto their heads as if it was a hot summer day, and they were trying to keep cool.

Once the individual started walking toward the crowd, the movement silenced everyone who spoke. No one talked or questioned one another until, off in the distance, the loud sound of police sirens shattered the midnight air. It awakened the people from the nosey stupor that zombified them so much that they would stand out in the pouring rain just to get a glimpse of a corpse lying in the middle of the street.

The police were on their way, and the closer they became, the farther away from the body everyone moved...so much that the number of individuals outside started to decrease. Everyone had the same question running through their minds, but no one wanted to get close enough to find out. The fingers began to point without anyone lifting a hand. There was no bench or jury trial needed because the looks that they gave showed how much they were convicting one another without any evidence. And while everyone immediately became distant, the still, lifeless body that laid on the hard wet cement had put the same thought into everyone's head. There was no innocent until proven guilty: everyone was guilty. Everyone was a suspect, and everyone had a motive. And everyone wanted to know if this was really Kelly, and if so, who killed her?

ACKNOWLEDGMENTS

I owe thanks to so many. First, a thank you to those of you who provide continuous support by purchasing my books. Thank you for your encouragement, your ideas, and your feedback.

Many thanks to Colby Kephart and the supportive team of Palmetto Publishing for creating such a platform that allows me to make my writings public.

I am also grateful to my first reader—Riyona Abraham, my niece, who is an avid reader. Her ability to read my manuscript and provide feedback in the quickest turnaround time that I've ever seen was exemplary.

A heartfelt thanks to my family and friends for their support and for the constant questioning of "when will the next book be available?"

To my daughter, THE QUEEN HERSELF, Ke'ara D. Sanders. My Keesa, I thank you for the idea. The day you came up with this idea while we were on one of our many lunch dates didn't fall on deaf ears. Your idea married with my ideas made the book we now hold in our hands titled *Coffee*.

To my son, MY Personal Stretch Armstrong, Alonzo Sanders Jr.
Thank you, son. Your insight and quirkiness are what has kept—and what keep me going.

And of course, I couldn't have written the book at all without the support of my husband, Alonzo Sanders Sr. Hats off to you, dear. Your behind-the-scenes work, managing me, pushing me, and pulling me goes beyond what anyone could ever imagine. I LOVE YOU!

Printed in the USA
CPSIA information can be obtained
at www.ICGtesting.com
LVHW091459271023
762201LV00012B/1468